Channeling Audrey Hepburn

The Romantic Misadventure of a Lifetime

D. M. MACKINNON

A POST HILL PRESS BOOK
ISBN: 979-8-88845-226-4
ISBN (eBook): 979-8-88845-227-1

Channeling Audrey Hepburn:
The Romantic Misadventure of a Lifetime

Cover illustration by Dolores Daly Flessner
Cover design by Jim Villaflores

Post Hill Press
New York • Nashville
posthillpress.com

Published in the United States of America
1 2 3 4 5 6 7 8 9 10

My mother Marie as well as Maureen
and Janice. Best Friends Forever.
And to Audrey Hepburn, whose style, elegance,
and kindness are needed now more than ever.

Chapter One

Patricia Ryan gently placed her head covered in stylishly short black hair in her hands and wept silently in the tiny cubicle which comprised her entire universe of space at the mid-size law firm of *Donovan, Miller, & O'Reilly* strategically located on Tremont Street in the heart of Boston.

While crying silently, she was also mindful to do it ever so quickly so as not to make things even worse for herself. Minutes earlier, Gerald Donovan – THE Donovan from *Donovan, Miller & O'Reilly* – had stepped out of his massive "I'm better than you and don't you ever forget it" corner office to dump three more assignments upon the slight shoulders of his legal secretary.

For Patricia, it wasn't the fact that the fifty-six year old name partner had no personality, or that he thought she was less than human or even the fact that like every assignment he gave her he expected it immediately, but rather that Gerald

Donovan was but one of *five* attorneys she now had to assist at a law firm where the capital partners averaged close to one million dollars per person in salary and bonus while paying the NTKs – or "non-time-keepers" – as little as they could legally get away with.

Almost universally, the lawyers – from associates to partners – had at least some degree of resentment toward the NTKs because they did not generate any income for the firm by billing the $200 to $800 dollars per hour like the lawyers, but rather simply took their relatively meager salaries while working cruelly-long and highly unappreciated hours. A fair amount of the partners truly felt that the money they paid to the NTKs was money out of their pockets come year-end bonus time. If they could get away with it, they would try to compensate their administrative assistants solely in "free" coffee and day-old pizza.

Coming from a very humble background, Patricia fully understood that her salary – however small compared to the ridiculous salaries and bonuses the partners awarded themselves—was still enviable for the millions of people in the country still struggling in a tough economy, or worse, unemployed.

That said, Donovan and three of her other four assigned partners bellowed at her and belittled her on a regular basis while simultaneously overworking her to the total of about 60 hours per week. Towards the end of the billing year when the partners were in overdrive to get cash in the door, Patricia and her fellow legal secretaries often worked 80 mind-numbing and spirit-breaking hours per week.

Fortunately for Patricia, there was an exception to this abuse by the name of Tom Harris. Harris was one of the five lawyers she had to assist but he was also about the kindest attorney she had ever met. Of course, for some, making that observation about a partner was like saying one was the nicest vulture in group circling high above your prostrate and almost lifeless body lying on an arid desert floor.

Still, the newly hired forty-year-old Harris *always* asked how she was doing, *always* smiled at her, and *always* asked if she had time to help him out. His hazel-green eyes always seemed to convey warmth and even a degree of sympathy gift-wrapped in genuine guilt for her plight.

For Patricia Ryan – or "PR" as most of the other legal secretaries called her – the grueling schedule inflicted upon her by the other four lawyers meant starting her workdays at about 8 AM and leaving for home exhausted usually at 8 or 9 PM.

Today – or now tonight – being one of those usual days. It was just after 8 PM when she finally finished the last of the assignments given to her by Donovan. Not that he would have noticed as he was long gone having left promptly at 6 PM to head over to the Boston Ballet with his wife and the other two-name partners—Terrance O'Reilly and Dan Miller.

By the time Patricia exited the office tower from the firm's 26th floor perch, the skies had opened drenching most of Boston in a warm July downpour. As she stood under the overhang just outside the two revolving doors of the office tower, her dark brown eyes moved back and forth in search of an open taxi. Normally, she would have walked the few blocks to the State Street "T" subway station, but today called for a sturdy ocean-liner or at the very least, an empty cab.

As anyone who lives in a big city knows, getting a taxi in a thunderstorm is akin to winning a state lottery. Actually, winning the lottery is *dramatically* easier.

Five minutes into her fruitless search, Patricia shook her head, pulled her pink knock-off *Prada* umbrella out of her brown knock-off *Louis Vuitton* handbag, and started her slosh toward the State-Street "T" stop.

Ironically, fifty-feet from the entrance of the subway stop, Patricia did encounter a taxi when it sped through a large lake-like puddle next to her and covered her from head to soaked shoes in grime-laced water.

"Perfect" she muttered to herself as she marched behind the other lemmings entering the station.

Chapter Two

7:45 the next morning found Patricia Ryan standing in line at the *Dunkin'* two blocks from her office waiting to order her desperately needed coffee.

As she shuffled her trim and quite shapely five-foot seven-inch body up one spot in line, the hand of a very attractive blonde reached out from behind and grabbed her right shoulder.

"Hey, PR." Said Maureen Ennis, her best friend since childhood and a fellow colleague at the firm. "What time last night were you able to slip your chains and get home?"

Patricia turned to face Maureen and looked at her through still blurry and tired eyes. "Oh, about 8:15 or so."

"You poor baby," answered Ennis – or "Mo" as Patricia called her—as she patted her friend on the shoulder. "And exactly what time did the Silver Skunk drop last night's '*I need it right this second*' project on you?"

The "Silver Skunk" was the legal assistant's nickname for Gerald Donovan who had a full-head of thick grey hair with a lighter patch running down the middle of his head.

Patricia covered her mouth as she tried to stifle a yawn. "Right around 6 PM. Just before he flew out the door with the others for their private box at the ballet."

Patricia and Mo then made it to the front of the line.

"I'll have a large 'Regular' coffee, please." Said Patricia to the perpetually smiling Juanita behind the counter.

As all proper Bostonians knew – and visitors sometimes learned – a "Regular Coffee" was Boston-talk for a coffee with half & half and two sugars added.

Mo next stepped up and looked at her best friend of over twenty years. "Don't you want a breakfast sandwich or something, Sweetie?"

As the still smiling Juanita handed her the coffee, Patricia looked at Mo's bright and clear blue eyes and shook her head.

"I barely have the strength to sip my coffee. Chewing food at this point is well beyond my capabilities."

As they exited the elevator on the 26th floor and prepared to head to their opposite corners of the building-wide floor, Patricia suddenly showed a quick flash of enthusiasm and energy.

"I just remembered that the *Audrey Hepburn* film festival under the stars starts tonight in Boston Common. We're still going, right?"

Mo adjusted her shoulder length blonde hair, smiled, and looked caringly at her friend who was as beautiful as she was insecure.

Being her best friend, Mo also knew what most in the firm did not. That aside from a social-life robbing work schedule, Patricia was also overwhelmed at home by a mother and grandmother who had chronic medical issues and often required Patricia to care for them when either the visiting nurse could not show up, or when money was tight and they declined the care. Both were on disability and shared Patricia's first-floor apartment in a triple-decker in West Roxbury.

As Maureen and Patricia had grown up in the Dorchester section of Boston – as in the hometown of actor *Mark Wahlberg* among others – and had by plan and coincidence always followed each other to employers and neighborhoods, Maureen grew to marvel at her friend who put up with so much and almost never complained as she consistently put others before her.

Though all the hardship and turmoil, Maureen and many others saw in Patricia what she did not see in herself.

That being that she had grown into a truly beautiful and elegant twenty-seven-year-old young woman of intelligence, style, grace, and charm.

As Mo prepared to answer, her smile became wider with the ironic knowledge that her best friend had more than a passing resemblance to Audrey Hepburn in her prime.

"Of course, we're going." Laughed Ennis. "No way I'm going to miss your stunning face up on the silver screen."

Patricia immediately put her finger to her lips. "Shhhh. Please don't start *that* again. I look nothing like Audrey Hepburn."

"Whatever you say...*Eliza Doolittle.* What time do you want to meet downstairs tonight?"

Patricia's face tightened with worry.

"With any luck, by 6:30 or so...If Mr. Donovan does not pile more work on me again."

Mo shook her head. "Don't worry. It's Friday. It ain't gonna happen. He usually leaves the firm at 2 PM for his foursome at his country club. You should be okay tonight, kiddo."

"I hope so," smiled Ryan. "Tonight, they are showing *Sabrina* and *Roman Holiday* and I've never seen either on the big screen."

"Well, you will tonight. Not to worry."

Chapter Three

Patricia stared blankly at her computer screen and realized she had not typed any words nor done any work for almost five minutes. She was getting the 3 PM drowsies and needed her afternoon hit of coffee to keep her head from eventually bouncing off her keyboard.

For a mid-size firm in a world of ever-expanding mega-firms, *Donovan, O'Reilly & Miller* was still quite successful. And like many successful firms, the partners sought to pamper their associates as much as possible so they could also overwork them just as much as they did the legal secretaries.

Because the "Associates" were the lowest form of lawyer at the firm – but still well above the NTKs on the firm food chain—they did the *vast majority* of legal work. This was primarily for two reasons. First, because *all* clients wanted to get the most bang out of their buck and did not want to get over-billed – or "ripped-off" – by sky-high billing partners. As first or second year lawyers billed the least amount per hour, the partners always made them do the bulk of the work so as not to upset the clients with obscenely high bills. The second reason the associates did most of the legal work was because many of the partners had become fat and lazy and preferred to do as little work as possible for their million or so dollars per year.

At least at *Donovan, Miller & O'Reilly.*

The partners were at least smart enough to know that if you were going to demand associates – or "The Inmates" as many of them called the rookie lawyers—to work upwards of two thousand billable hours per year, you had better give them a few of the creature comforts of life. One of those creature comforts being a nice kitchen and in-house cafe stocked with all kinds of "free" goodies like coffee, cookies, and the occasional hot meal.

Even though the kitchens and small cafes – the firm had three per floor in the two floors they occupied in the office tower – were primarily created to keep the inmates happy, the legal secretaries were also – quite reluctantly as far as the partners were concerned – allowed to use them.

The only reason the partners did not completely bar the legal secretaries from the kitchens and cafes was their paranoid fear of a class-action lawsuit being filed against them.

That said, what the legal secretaries and most others did not know was that the capital partners got even with the legal secretaries by unethically deducting a set amount of money from the tiny year-end bonus paid to each legal secretary as a way to punish them for *daring* to drink the "free" coffee or having the occasional cookie.

As Patricia rounded the corner of the little kitchen/cafe just down the hall from her desk, she found Tom Harris putting the same dollar bill in and out of the candy machine while muttering to himself about technology and worn-out money.

"Hi, Mr. Harris," said Patricia as she walked behind the frustrated partner.

Harris turned around as Patricia passed him. "Oh, hi, Patty." He then stopped in mid-sentence. "I'm sorry. I'm still new around here. Do you prefer Patty, Patricia, or something else?"

Patricia was honestly surprised that he even knew her name let alone stop to ask what she preferred to be called.

"Well…I like 'Patricia,' but 'Patty' is okay if you would rather call me that."

"No way," smiled Harris. "Patricia it shall be."

"Thank you." Smiled Ryan in turn.

"Okay," continued Harris. "Since we have established that, I have a small favor to ask you."

"Yes," squinted Ryan as she was not used to having this much human contact with partners.

"Since I have rightfully agreed to call you 'Patricia,' can you please call me Tom? As has been said in the past, the only 'Mr. Harris' I know is my dad."

"Alright…Tom," the suddenly blushing legal secretary answered.

"Great. Since we have our names now all figured out, do you have four quarters for this worn-out dollar bill this candy machine seems to hate?"

Patricia shook her head.

"I don't have any quarters, but I do have some new dollar bills I got from the bank the other day. Would you like to try one of them?"

"Please," laughed Harris. "I have a craving for a Milky Way bar even though I'm trying to watch my waistline."

While trying not to do so, Patricia took a quick glance at Harris's waistline and saw no evidence that he had anything to worry about. All the opposite.

While in the ladies' room the other day, she had overheard two of the other legal secretaries talking about the new partner and that "he was in great shape." She found nothing to disagree with their assessment.

Harris had come over to *Donovan, O'Reilly & Miller* a month ago from a competing firm in Boston and had brought six other attorneys with him. Since arriving, he had also become the subject of some speculation and gossip as he was still single at forty and considered by most women to be "beyond handsome."

Patricia handed the six-foot three-inch lawyer a new dollar bill and watched as he inserted the money, and the machine hungrily accepted it.

As if in a trance, she heard her own voice suddenly blurt-out "your waistline looks fine to me" as if she were having an out-of-body experience.

Now it was Harris's turn to blush. A result which made Ryan feel even more uncomfortable.

"I'm so sorry I said that Mr. Harris."

"Tom…remember?" Smiled Harris at her. "And don't worry about it. I started that conversation."

He then looked down at his flat-stomach. "Actually, a candy bar is usually something I don't eat. As I said, I just had a weird craving and I'm pretty sure I'm not even pregnant."

They both forced-chuckled at his predictable and unfunny joke before a bit of an awkward silence settled-in.

To break that silence, Harris suddenly said, "I normally like to run a few miles every morning and play the occasional game of tennis when my schedule allows. What about you?"

Ryan tried not to laugh out loud at the question as she thought –*are you kidding me? With the hours you partners make me work, I'm lucky I have time to brush my teeth let alone get in a game of tennis or squash with the other "chaps" at Harvard.*

That's what she thought. What she said was: "I'm really not much of a sports person. I like to walk as much as possible, but when I do walk, it's usually to museums or in search of old film festivals."

"You like old movies?" Asked Harris as he slipped the Milky War bar into the front pocket of his crisp white French-collar shirt.

"I do."

"Then you probably know that there is an Audrey Hepburn film festival starting tonight on the Common."

"I do, thank you. I plan to go with my best-friend if..." Her voice then trailed off as she realized she barely knew the man, that he was a senior partner at the firm, and that she didn't want to cross any lines by saying too much.

Harris was quick enough to realize where she was going and finished the sentence for her as he adjusted the clearly expensive solid gold-yellow tie giving his shirt a splash of color.

"...If those slave-driving partners don't give you too much work before you try and head out the door."

Patricia gave off the hint of a faint and knowing smile as she turned her gaze and faced toward the floor.

"Well," Harris continued. "I can guarantee you that *this* partner won't give you any last-minute assignments tonight and *almost* guarantee that your other four attorneys won't as well."

Patricia looked back up and smiled at Harris. "That's very nice of you to say...even if it doesn't quite work out that way."

"Oh, it will." Answered Harris as he ran his hand through his thick black hair.

Ryan nodded. "Well, speaking of work, I had better get my fix of caffeine and get back to my desk if I hope to get out in time for the first movie tonight."

Tom Harris returned the nod as he started to leave the kitchen. Three steps into his exit he stopped and turned back to face Patricia.

"Speaking of Audrey Hepburn...has anyone ever told you that..."

Patricia laughed as she held up her hand in the "Stop" position. "Please don't even go there. Let's not insult the memory of one of the most beautiful and elegant women of all time."

Harris stood and looked Patricia in the eye for a full three-count before saying, "Oh, I'm not...See you around, Patricia."

Chapter Four

As promised by Tom Harris and Mo, Patricia was able to make the film festival on time.

Both she and Maureen were surprised to find the outdoor movie theater on the Boston Common packed with people. Mostly "female" people.

After the first film *Sabrina* ended, almost half of those in attendance headed toward the exits. As they did so, Patricia and Mo grabbed their blanket and moved closer and more toward the center so as to have a better view of the next film which was *Roman Holiday* – Patricia's all-time favorite movie.

"Dinner time," announced Mo as she opened up a plastic bag and pulled out a twelve-inch Turkey *Subway* sandwich and a sixteen-ounce plastic bottle of *Coke.*

While she did this, Patricia opened an elegant little picnic basket and removed a small bottle of Pinot noir coupled with a sliced French-baguette, duck pate, and a tiny-wheel of chevre-Cheese.

She next removed two small plates along with two wine glasses, cloth napkins and silverware for two.

As she did all this, Mo just sat with a smile, which grew to a giggle, before finally morphing into a full-throated laugh.

"Gee," said Mo. "Let's look at my selection for dinner under the stars and then look at yours and decide which of these women is out of place at an *Audrey Hepburn* film festival."

"Well," answered Patricia as she prepared a plate for Mo. "If you keep your burping to a minimum, I don't think most people will notice that you slipped by the etiquette police to land on my oh-so-perfect blanket."

Towards the end of *Roman Holiday* when *Joe Bradley* as played by Gregory Peck and *Princess Ann* as played by Audrey Hepburn discovered their love for each other while sitting in the tiny Italian car outside the gates of the palace, Patricia turned to Mo and grabbed her arm.

As she continued to squeeze, Mo finally said "Owwww' as she pulled her arm free and began rubbing it.

"What's up with the vice-like grip, Hercules," she whispered to Patricia as *Joe Bradley* and *Princess Ann* kissed and embraced in the front seat of the car.

"Oh, I'm so sorry," said Patricia after realizing what she had done. "I just had an amazing thought. Sort of like an epiphany."

Mo continued to rub her arm. "Must have been a heck of a thought."

"I think it might be...at least for me." Whispered Patricia back at Mo. "I will tell you all about it over coffee in my kitchen when we get home."

After taking the "T" and a bus back to the West Roxbury section of Boston, Mo sat at the kitchen table in Patricia's small apartment while Patricia went about making them some coffee.

Mo looked over and watched as Patricia spooned some coffee out of a brown and black bag.

"What kind of coffee is that?" Asked Mo.

"It's called *Peet's*. It is from Seattle but much better than *Starbucks*. It's really exceptional. This one is their French-Roast brand."

"And what's wrong with good old *Dunkin'* coffee, Miss Sophisticated?"

"Nothing," answered Patricia as she pushed the button to start the brewing process. "Sometimes I just like to try something new. What's wrong with that?"

Mo smiled over at her. "Nothing at all, Sweetie. Even though it's late, I'll have some since I am wide awake. Now why don't you tell me all about your epiphany."

Just as Patricia was putting the coffee cups, sugar and half & half on the table, her mother Anna walked out of the kitchen wearing a thick blue bathrobe and white slippers.

"Labored" rather than "walked" would have been a better choice of words. Because of scoliosis operation which did not go as well as hoped at a Boston Hospital two years earlier, combined with degenerating disks in the spine, the fifty-four-year-old woman navigated her way toward the kitchen table by holding the counter and the side of the refrigerator along the way as she failed in her attempt to hide her pain and wincing from her daughter and Maureen.

"Hi, girls," smiled the still attractive heavier, shorter, and twenty-seven years older version of Patricia as she quickly settled into a chair. "I thought I heard your voices out here. How was the film festival?"

Patricia smiled quickly at Mo before answering.

"Oh, it was great, Mom. It was so wonderful to see Audrey Hepburn up on the big screen like that for the first time."

Since Patricia was ten years of age, she and her mom had shared a special bond regarding Audrey Hepburn and her movies. It was right about that time, that her dad John, who worked for the Post Office at the General Mail Facility in South Boston, had come home and admitted to her mom that he was "in love" with a female colleague at the post office and that he was moving out that very day to be with her.

Patricia was a very bright and aware ten-year-old and knew something bad had transpired even though her mom and dad had gone to their bedroom, closed the door, and kept their voices low.

Ten minutes after she had gone in, Patricia's mom came out and sat at the kitchen table facing a wall while continually dabbing her eyes with a tissue while trying to not make a sound.

Ten minutes after that, Patricia's dad walked out of the bedroom with a full suitcase, looked at Patricia for a few seconds with some degree of real sadness in his eyes, hugged her, and then quickly walked out of the apartment softly closing the door behind him.

That very night, *American Movie Classics* was showing the film "*How to Steal a Million*" with Audrey Hepburn and Peter O'Toole. Patricia's mom asked her if she would sit and watch it with her and Patricia instantly agreed knowing her mom needed her now more than ever.

Sitting on their small worn-out sofa in their then, two-bedroom apartment near Columbia Road in Dorchester, Patricia watched her very first Audrey Hepburn movie on a black & white television as she and her mom shared a bowl of popcorn.

From that moment forward, anytime one of them was down, they would rent, stream, and watch an Audrey Hepburn movie while talking about life in general and pray and *pretend* that things would all be better soon.

"What were the movies at the festival tonight?" asked Patricia's mom.

"*Sabrina* and *Roman Holiday.*" Answered Mo as she reached over and squeezed the hand of her "second" mom.

"Oh, I love them both," smiled Mrs. Ryan. "What are they showing tomorrow night?"

"*My Fair Lady* and *How to Steal a Million.*" Answered Patricia as she filled Mo's coffee cup.

Once finished, she touched her mother on the shoulder.

"Would you like some coffee, mom?"

Her mother shook her head. "Oh, no thank you, sweetheart. I just wanted to come out to say goodnight and that I love you both."

"We love you, too," said Patricia and Mo at the same time as they then laughed at the timing.

Mo then watched with more than a little sadness as Patricia stood before her mom, grasped her hands, and pulled her mother gently and slowly into a standing position for about the one-thousandth time. Mo knew that Mrs. Ryan was still too proud to use the walker the hospital had given her but also knew it was just a matter of time.

Once Mrs. Ryan was standing, Patricia and Mo each gave her a kiss on the cheek as Patricia walked her back down the hallway to her bedroom.

Chapter Five

Two minutes later, Patricia was sitting back before Mo at the table with her eyes still ablaze from whatever "epiphany" she had while watching "*Roman Holiday.*"

"Okay, so tell me already." Said Mo. "What's the big and mysterious idea you had at the movies tonight?"

"Promise you won't laugh."

Mo shook her head. "No way. Laughing in your face is my right as your very best friend if you tell me something totally stupid."

Some of the fire went out of Patricia's eyes. "Well then, maybe I shouldn't tell you."

Mo let out an exasperated breath. "Fine. I promise to *try* and not laugh in your face. Is *that* good enough?"

Patricia's eyes went back to full incandescence. "Good enough."

Before continuing, she watched as Mo took a sip of the coffee.

"First," smiled Patricia. "How do you like the coffee?"

Mo shrugged her shoulders. "I must admit it's very good. Much better than I thought. Why? Is this all part of your 'broaden my horizons' project?"

"Something like that."

"Well, good luck with that. Now that we are finished with tonight's culinary part of the program, can you finally tell me about your brainstorm?"

Patricia wrapped both hands around her coffee cup as if searching for warmth even though it was the middle of July.

"Well…as we were watching the end of *Roman Holiday*, I started to think '*wouldn't it be nice to be Audrey Hepburn for a few days*.'"

Mo let out a quick laugh before stifling the rest in honor of her promise.

"You're not exactly blazing any new trails with that thought, Daniel Boone. I think about one hundred million women beat you to the punch."

Patricia smiled back at Mo. "I know. But that's *not* what I'm getting at."

"It's not?" Said Mo as she caught the glint of mischievousness in her friend's eyes.

"No. Not even remotely close," continued Patricia. "As you know…way better than anyone…my life has been a bit of a challenge these last few years…"

Patricia then quickly turned her head toward her mom's bedroom and saw that the door was closed, but still lowered her voice to almost a whisper.

"...every day for the last few months, I feel more and more lost. I'm not sure what the clinical definition of depression is, but I must be at least getting close. I'm going to be twenty-eight years old in October and I'm starting to think I'm never going to meet the right man, and never going to get the chance to have a..."

Patricia stopped as her eyes again filled with tears. Something which was happening more and more frequently while serving as a bright red flag of warning to Patricia that her mind was entering unchartered territory.

"Sorry," she smiled as she looked up at Mo's face, while taking a napkin from the table to wipe her tears.

"Don't be." Answered Mo. "Or have you forgotten that I'm also in the same 'why have I not found Mr. Right' boat as you."

Patricia suddenly felt guilty that Mo might be thinking her thoughts were selfish. "Oh, never. I'm so sorry. It's just you are so much better at dealing with it than me."

Maureen shook her head. "Maybe I'm just a better actress. So don't worry. Continue telling me about your idea."

Patricia took a deep breath and then a long sip of coffee. When done, she blinked a few times before going on.

"...Well, again, as you know better than any, life at the firm is miserable. They have succeeded in turning me into some kind of zombie. I get up at 6 AM, shower, take the "T," have a coffee, work ten to twelve hours a day...or more...get back on the "T," grab a quick bite, check on Mom and Nana, collapse in bed and then do it all over again the next day. Day after day. Week after week, and now, year after year. If it wasn't because of my mom and grandmother..."

Patricia felt her eyes fill again but this time went on talking.

"…I would have quit that place a long time ago."

"I know, Sweetie." Said Mo as she patted her friend's hand. "Because I work in human resources, I don't have to deal with the slave drivers you have, and I *only* have to work about fifty hours a week or so. Also, I have a very healthy mom and dad who can take care of themselves. All of that said, I'm not far behind you in feeling lost…and…lonely. In the best of times, it's almost impossible to meet a good and decent man."

Patricia nodded and wrapped her hand around her friend's.

"I know. Well…one of the good things about the hundreds of extra hours they have forced me to work – most likely illegally – is that I have been able to save some money."

"How much?" Asked Mo.

Patricia lowered her voice even more. "About fifteen thousand dollars. Enough to take a leave of absence for a couple of months and still have money to pay the bills around here for mom and nana."

Mo raised her eyebrows and smiled. "Take a leave of absence for …*what*?"

Patricia wiped her eyes again but then smiled wider than her friend. "Back to the subject of Audrey Hepburn."

Mo held up a finger. "Before you continue, I want you to know that whatever it is, I am with you. I am, after all, your best friend. If you need me to go with you, I'm there. Whatever it is, I'm in. Period."

"I'm so very happy to hear you say that. So…my plan… and I'm obviously still working out all the kinks…is not to *be*

Audrey Hepburn, but rather, to go and *recreate* some of the most adventurous scenes of her *characters*."

"*What* does that all mean? Like what?" Asked Mo as she wrinkled her forehead a bit in anticipation of the answer.

Patricia jumped up from the table from the force of her pent-up energy and excitement.

"I don't know. I don't know. Maybe like going to Paris, finding a great looking young man, and convincing him to help me *pretend* to rob a museum like in the movie "*How to Steal a Million*." To just go on the adventure of a lifetime before life manages to beat me down anymore than it already has. What do you say? Are you still in?"

It was now Mo's turn to jump up from the table.

"Are you *actually* serious?"

Patricia put her fingers to her lips and nodded nervously.

"I think so. Yes…I am. Never more serious. Are you in?"

Mo took a step back and shook her head vigorously. "Are you crazy? I'm out."

Surprisingly, Patricia smiled even more with her friend's answer. As if certitude and peace had finally lifted the invisible but crushing weight from her weary shoulders.

Chapter Six

7:45 AM the next morning, Patricia walked into the kitchen down the hall from her cubicle balancing a bulging red-well legal folder, a medium coffee from *Dunkin'*, a bagel and a side of cream-cheese, and her purse.

Just as all of them started to slip from her trembling hands onto the floor, she made it to one of the three round tables in the sitting area of the kitchen. As soon as she was six inches from the grey table surrounded by four white plastic cafeteria chairs, she let the ultra-heavy file folder tumble from her fingers so as to save the coffee and the bagel.

Naturally, the folder bounced off the table, ricocheted down to one of the chairs, and then plopped onto the floor where the elastic band holding the folder closed, snapped off with a loud POP, allowing the overflow of papers to shoot out all over the floor with the majority coming to rest under the table.

For a full ten seconds, Patricia just looked down at the mess around her feet as if in a trance. After the ten-second mark, she ever so slowly placed the coffee, the bagel, the cream cheese, and her purse on the table. Then, just as slowly, she walked around to the other side of the table, pulled out a white chair, sat in it, and stared at the mess on the floor as her eyes started to water.

Thirty seconds after that...Tom Harris walked in.

As soon as Patricia saw him, she bolted out of the chair so fast it clattered behind her as she ran from the kitchen toward the ladies' room.

Five minutes later after washing her face and sort-of composing herself, she walked back into the kitchen to find Tom Harris now sitting at the table with all her papers neatly back in the red-well folder which was back on top of the table alongside her coffee and bagel.

"Thank you, Mr. Harris," Patricia said just above a whisper as she looked at a spot on the floor between her and Tom Harris.

"Tom," replied Harris. "You promised. Remember?"

"Tom," answered a still red-faced Ryan. "I'm so very sorry for running out like that."

Harris stood up and pulled out a chair for Patricia.

She looked at him and then at the chair, nodded to herself as if making an important decision, and then gently sat down.

"No need to apologize." Smiled Harris as he pushed the chair in behind her. "I'm guessing the file hitting the floor was the proverbial straw that broke the camel's back."

Patricia managed a small but genuine smile. "Something like that."

"Listen," said Harris still standing. "I've got to go prepare for a conference call with my favorite client from Japan, but I was wondering if you might let me buy you lunch later today?"

Patricia looked up at him and while still embarrassed that he caught her melting down a bit, she could not help but notice how impeccable and handsome he looked. From his sharply creased navy-blue slacks, to his crisp white shirt, to his bold red tie. She thought he looked like Hollywood's version of a leading man instead of the highly successful lawyer in Boston that he was.

Patricia also simply appreciated the fact that Harris dressed in a suit every day for work. Years ago, because of the dot com business craze where all the 20 something millionaires dressed like slobs, law firms – in order to be competitive with the dot com companies – expanded "casual Friday's" into "casual every day," with the expected result.

While coming from no money and having next to no money, Patricia still greatly prized class, elegance, and as much fashion as she could afford. Even if it was "Knock-off" fashion.

As she often told Mo, "Style is important. Fashion is important. Women need to 'Dress for Success' just as much – or even more – than men."

Patricia had always felt that the workplace—as well as when one went out in public – called for one to dress as well and as elegantly as possible. She understood she was in the minute minority on this issue but still felt strongly about it.

Patricia had always felt that the more you paid attention to fashion and the more elegant you dressed for work, the better your work ethic became and the higher your confidence rose. Conversely, she believed as the partners and lawyers moved further and further away from wearing suits to the office – and she swore a few of them had basically worn their pajamas to the firm a few times – the more their work product and work ethic suffered.

Naturally, if the work product or work ethic of the partners and associates suffered, they would find some reason to place the blame squarely upon their legal secretaries and heap more work on top of the crushing burden they had already given them.

After her micro-second inspection of Harris – whose work product and work ethic never suffered—Patricia smiled again while shaking her head. “Sorry, Tom. That’s very kind, but I brought my lunch today.”

“Perfect,” answered Harris without missing a beat and a smile wide enough to trump Ryan’s. “I brought mine as well, so how about 1 PM on a park bench in the Common overlooking the frog pond?”

Patricia now laughed. “That’s still very nice but I was going to stay at my desk today.” She waved at the red-well folder as she continued. “I’m way behind…as usual.”

Harris shook his head. “No, I don’t think so. Not as long as I’m a partner in this firm. Enough of you giving your life to this place. It’s not worth it. In fact, I want to discuss the firm with you over lunch so please reconsider and allow me the pleasure of being a cheapskate and sharing a free lunch with you on bird-stained park bench.”

“Well,” answered Patricia with now the glimmer of a twinkle in her eyes. “Since you put it that way…okay. That would be wonderful. But still under one condition if you don't mind."

"And what might that be?"

Patricia suddenly felt an unexpected surge of confidence. A feeling that comes when you have finally cracked the code to an overwhelming problem.

As Tom Harris looked at her expectantly, he noticed that a light seemed to come alive in her dark and troubled eyes.

Patricia now stood and smoothed her clothes. An outfit she had put together to try and replicate the style and elegance of her favorite designer, Givenchy.

"The condition being that I *meet* you at the park bench."

Harris laughed. "Really? That's it? That's your condition? Why? Are you ashamed to be seen with me in public?"

Patricia walked over to the sink and poured her now lukewarm coffee down the drain. When finished, she turned back to face Harris.

"Not ashamed at all, Tom. I simply choose not to become idol gossip for some of the smaller-minded partners and attorneys around here who have turned speculating about the lives of their colleagues and assistants into a very hurtful full-contact sport."

"Wow," said a suddenly intrigued Harris. "This is a tougher side of you."

"Maybe," smiled Patricia to lighten the mood. "I had an epiphany of sorts yesterday, and it's starting to become more real to me."

Harris raised his dark eyebrows. "Something you can share with me at lunch?"

"I will think about it," laughed Ryan. "But only *after* you meet me at the bench."

"Oh, yeah," smiled Harris as he started to walk out of the kitchen. "Because you're ashamed to be seen with me in public. I think I'll go call my mom and tell her that."

Mo was reviewing updated information to the firm's healthcare plan when the phone on her desk rang. She quickly looked down and saw that it was coming from Patricia's extension.

"Hey, PR." Said Mo as she ran a yellow highlighter across a section of the healthcare plan which pointed out that even *more* benefits were being taken away from the administrative assistants and all those who did not bill time for the firm. "What's up?"

"Red alert!" Blurted out Ryan. "I think I just made a big mistake and I need to talk to you right away."

Mo put the yellow highlighter down and devoted her full attention to the phone and her best friend.

"Don't tell me you just quit the firm."

"Oh, no." Said Patricia. "It's much worse than that. I just agreed to go to lunch with Tom Harris."

Mo let out a loud whistle. "The hot looking new partner?"

"Shhhhhhh..." pleaded Ryan before continuing. "...you think he's hot?"

"Smoking." Answered Mo with a laugh.

"Well," said Ryan as she lowered her voice. "It doesn't matter what he is. It was a moment on temporary insanity on my part and I'm going to cancel."

"Women's room…two minutes," commanded Mo in a loud voice as she hung up the phone before Patricia could reply.

As Patricia walked into the ladies' room closest to her section of the office, she noticed Mo pushing open the door to the last stall and looking inside.

Mo then turned and saw Patricia. "Okay. We're alone. Spill it. What's your major malfunction on this one?"

Patricia suddenly felt a little flush and turned on the cold water in one of the sinks and splashed some of the water on her reddening face.

After drying herself with a paper towel, she leaned against the sink and answered the friend who always had her back.

"I don't know. I barely know Tom Harris and he asks me to go to lunch. Don't you think that's a bit odd?"

"Odd?" Laughed Mo.

She then walked over to Patricia, grabbed her by the shoulders and turned her so they were both facing the mirror. "Maybe you need to be reminded how truly *beautiful* you are. Take a look in the mirror and you will see *nothing* odd about Mr. Harris asking you to lunch."

Patricia looked at herself for two seconds and then shifted her eyes to look at Mo's reflection in the mirror before answering the reverse image of her friend.

"First, I'm nothing special…"

Mo let out an immediate grunt and shook her head in disagreement.

"...and second," Patricia said in a somewhat louder voice. "I don't think Tom is like that..."

"*Tom*?" Interjected Mo with a smile.

"Yes," answered Patricia. "He asked me to call him 'Tom.'"

"Oh, okay," smiled Mo. "No way the ultra-handsome male partner who asked you to call him '*Tom*,' and asked you to lunch would do so because he's a *normal* red-blooded American male and thinks you are a stunningly beautiful woman...which you *are*, by the way."

Patricia allowed herself a smile at her friend's passionate sales job. "Well...he may be all of those things, but I especially think he's a very decent person more than anything else."

"Okay," laughed Mo. "But is there a law that says a decent and moral man can't ask out a woman who *also* happens to be decent and very moral?"

"No. I guess not," answered Patricia in a lowered voice.

"So what's your problem, then? Have lunch with the decent, moral, and incredibly handsome guy!"

Chapter Seven

With multiple thoughts bouncing about her head, Patricia dashed quickly out of the front door of her firm at 12:40 PM for the five-minute walk to Boston Common. With her, she carried her lunch in a small insulated green fabric cooler with the meal consisting of a small bottle of water, a small piece of salmon and a few green beans in a plastic container she had just heated in a microwave before leaving the office.

Ryan entered the Common from Tremont Street and proceeded to walk slightly uphill towards the Beacon Street side of the park where the frog pond was located. Once there, she found an empty bench with the bright gold dome of the State House behind her and the frog pond and a view of Tremont Street before her. Five seconds after sitting down, she spotted Tom Harris's tall and athletic frame entering the park from the same entrance she had just used. He was not wearing his suit coat on the 84-degree day in Boston, and his crisp white dress shirt and red tie seemed to sparkle from the light of the sun in the cloudless blue sky.

As she watched him make his way up the gradual incline on his five-minute journey toward her, she was pleased—and intrigued—to see him with a constant smile on his face—even as he dodged a few skateboarders and several strollers being pushed by moms who definitely turned to admire him once they had passed.

One minute away, he spotted Patricia sitting on the bench and waved with his smile growing ten-fold.

As she waved back, she suddenly felt her face flush again with warmth. *What's up with that*, she quickly asked herself as she stood to greet him.

"Wow," he said as he reached her and the weathered green bench and looked around the park. "We could not have picked a better day to escape the law factory."

"Yes," she answered somewhat apprehensively as her dark brown eyes shifted from Harris to the beauty of the Common before them. On this spectacular summer day, the green of the grass seemed greener, the blue of the sky seemed bluer, the temperature was perfect, and the laughs and sounds of the children playing around the frog pond were at a perfect volume. It could not have been a nicer day in the heart of Boston except for the fact that Patricia still had no idea why Tom had invited her out and that lack of knowledge made her both nervous and cautious.

"Where is your lunch?" Patricia suddenly asked as he looked down at the empty hands of Harris.

"Oh, here." Smiled Harris as he pulled a sandwich wrapped in cellophane out of one pants pocket and a small plastic bottle of orange juice out of the other.

Patricia burst out laughing as she sat down. "Men."

As Tom sat at the other end of the bench, she looked down at his somewhat squished sandwich which he was carefully trying to free from the cellophane.

"*What* is it?" She asked.

Harris smiled in triumph as he removed the last of the cellophane. "A peanut butter and jelly sandwich on white bread."

As nervous and cautious as she was, Patricia still could not help herself. "Wow. Peanut butter and Jelly. What kind of rotten financial deal did you get from the name partners? All the coffee you can drink and stale pizza you can eat from the lunchroom? If so, you are too late as that is *our* compensation plan from the firm."

It was Harris' turn to burst out laughing. "You saw my contract. How? It's supposed to be confidential."

He then looked down at her green cooler. "Okay. Now show me what you brought for our informal lunch on a dirty park bench in Boston Common."

Patricia shrugged her shoulders as she opened her small green cooler and removed a small bottle of Evian water, two white cloth napkins, silverware consisting of a small fork and knife, and then the plastic container holding her salmon and green beans. She then took one of the napkins and spread it out on the space between her and Harris on the bench and then placed her container in the center of her makeshift placemat.

Tom whistled softly. "I am both impressed by you… and…embarrassed at my barbaric manners."

Patricia shook her head. "Well, please don't be either." She then nodded at his mangled sandwich. "And please eat."

As Tom took a bite, Patricia continued.

"I guess in a way, I am a throw-back. I am a bit of an old-fashioned woman living in very *un-fashioned* times. Growing up, we never had much in the way of money or material wealth, but my mom strongly believed that just because we did not have as much as others, it was still not an excuse not to have manners, class and to be civil to those around us. I am my mother's daughter." Finished Patricia with a smile.

As Harris wiped his mouth with a crumpled paper napkin he had pulled out of his pocket, he smiled in response as he paused to admire the woman sitting across from him wearing a short-sleeved yellow blouse atop a Navy-blue, mid-calf pencil skirt, with a belt accentuated her small waist. All of which he noticed, while elegant, still highlighted – at least to his eyes – her perfect figure.

"Well, I agree with your mom, then. The world needs a great deal more elegance, class, and good manners."

Patricia now frowned as she finished chewing a small piece of salmon. "It's true, you know. I get it that some people at the firm may think I am too prim and proper. I also know that some think I am pretending to be something I am not. That I am acting as if I am part of the upper crust from *Beacon Hill* instead of one of the *unwashed masses* from real Boston. Well, I am not. I know who and what I am, and I am not the least bit ashamed of my status. All the opposite in fact. As my mom taught me, having and exhibiting elegance and class costs nothing. And as people seem to become ruder and more selfish in this increasingly crazy world, it makes me feel better to act in a way which is true to myself. And besides...I am not hurting anyone."

Harris looked at her for a few seconds with open admiration before answering. "No, you're not. Not at all. In fact, I find you and your attitude more refreshing and real than I can tell you. I also find you more candid and more open than I thought you'd be."

Patricia softly closed the lid of her plastic container. "Well, I am sorry about that. I didn't mean to be so open and honest. Most especially as we barely know each other. It's just that... well...two things. First, because of that epiphany I mentioned to you yesterday which, surprisingly to me, makes me much more willing to say exactly what is on my mind combined with the fact that I feel somehow, very comfortable in speaking with you."

Harris bowed toward her from his sitting position on the bench. "I am flattered that you feel that way. Now, before I mention why I wanted to drag you out to this park bench, do you want to share your epiphany with me?"

Chapter Eight

Patricia looked at his kind face and into his warm eyes and was honestly confused and *concerned* as to why she always felt instantly more at peace when in his presence. She did just barely know him and more importantly, knew next to nothing about him *or* his personal life.

She decided to throw caution to the wind and take a risk by opening up even more to a man she had just recently met. And it was a *real* risk, because for her to be honest, she knew she would have to be very critical of the firm to a man who was a senior partner in that very firm.

She waited for Harris to finish taking a sip of his orange juice before continuing. "It's not really that mysterious or that unusual actually. After a great deal of thought, I have decided to take a sabbatical from the firm."

Like all good lawyers, Harris had been trained to never ask a question to which he did not already know the answer.

"Oh, really. Why?" He asked with just a trace of a knowing smile on his face.

Patricia looked directly into his deep blue eyes for a few seconds before answering. "Can we keep this conversation strictly between us?"

Harris reached over and touched the back of her hand as he said, "I promise."

When his hand touched the back of hers, it felt as if a jolt of electricity had run up her arm. An experience she had never felt during her twenty-seven plus years on the planet.

Because of the feeling, she momentarily lost her train of thought and looked down at her skirt and straightened it while trying to compose herself.

After a few seconds of flattening imaginary wrinkles, she remembered what she wanted to say. "Thank you," she replied with a smile which now held several conflicting emotions. "The simple and most truthful answer is that I can't take it anymore. I honestly think a number of partners and associates at the firm not only take their incredibly hard-working legal secretaries for granted but abuse them on a regular basis. Both by the unfair amount of work they pile upon them daily as well as, and most especially damaging, the emotional and verbal abuse they constantly direct at them. As you witnessed this morning, it's all gotten to me, and I think it's proving very unhealthy to my mental and physical well-being."

Harris expected something like this, but not a full data-dump of pent-up emotions and frustration. Even though he knew he went out of his way to treat all assistants as his true equals, he still felt a wave of guilt wash over him with Ryan's answer.

Harris once again put his hand on Ryan's, and she once again felt the exact same surge as before.

"Patricia. I am so sorry about all of this. I…"

She gently slid her hand from under his so she could think and respond.

"Tom," she said as she now avoided looking into his eyes for the moment. "You have nothing to be sorry about. All the opposite. From the brief time we have known each other to what others in the firm say about you, I know that you are a good person and don't look upon the assistants as slaves to be used and abused."

"Thank you for saying that Patricia, but…"

Before Harris could finish his sentence, Ryan quickly continued.

"Sorry to interrupt, Tom. But I just want to get this out. I *need* to get this out. I am honestly amazed that I am sharing so much with you, but here we are. I also want you to know it's not just the firm. As bad as things are over there…" she said as she nodded her head in the direction of their office tower looming across the sunlit park. "…I also have a number of serious problems at home to deal with. I live with my disabled mom and grandmother – who I love beyond what words can express—and have also become, not only the primary support for both of them, but their primary caretaker as well. I know I could handle things if it was *just* my home situation or *just* the firm situation, but both have combined to overwhelm me. All of that coupled with the fact that I am single and must face it alone…"

Patricia stopped as her emotions got the better of her and she felt tears once again well-up in her eyes. She turned away from Harris as she tried to take some deep breaths and get things back in check.

As she did so, she was now not surprised to feel Harris wordlessly place her napkin in her left hand.

After quickly dabbing her eyes, she turned back on the bench to face Harris. "I am sorry about that. That is happening more and more frequently, and I seem to keep apologizing to you for the same thing. I am going to make sure that is the last time you have to see me like that."

Unexpectedly to her, Harris shook his head in response and smiled. "Why? Because you are acting like a very normal human being with very normal human feelings? As we talked about, I find it all refreshing and truthfully…hope inspiring in the sense that in an age where electronic communications between people dominates all, and human faces are constantly bathed in the inhuman white light of the offending devices most have become addicted to, I have come across a wonderfully real person not only not afraid to show her emotions, but one who actually *verbally* communicates."

Patricia felt a real burst of pride with Harris's words. "You do?'

"Absolutely," answered Harris. "If fact…and I had no plans to mention this, but it now seems in perfect context… while driving to the office this morning, I was trying to remember how many actual verbal words my fiancé and I have exchanged in the last week. She *lives* on her iPhone and texts and tweets seem to be her primary mode of communications these days…"

Patricia felt as if the world's *Mixed Martial Arts Champion* had just punched her in the stomach with all his might. The word "fiancé" was vibrating inside her head like an alarm bell gone crazy. Tom was still speaking to her, but his words were now distant and fuzzy.

What is wrong with you now, she asked herself as she desperately tried to act as if nothing had happened.

"...her name is Simone, and she is the new weekend anchor for Channel Five here in Boston with every intention of becoming the weeknight anchor just as quickly as possible. I am honestly starting to feel sorry for the person who now has that job."

"Uh, uh," was all Patricia could manage to say.

Harris did not seem to be aware of her dilemma as he had just made an important decision of his own.

"Look," he said as he sat up straighter on the bench while turning squarely to face her. "I have never done this in my life with someone I have also only just met, but I am going to get something off *my* chest if that is okay...especially seeing how you are a woman and might not only understand but have an explanation as well."

"Uh, uh," repeated Patricia as her mind was suddenly searching for the best way to end the conversation.

"Great," smiled the oblivious Harris. "I have known my fiancé for about three years. We met when I was working in Washington, DC and she was working for the ABC News affiliate down there. She comes from a great deal of money. Her grandparents came from France and created one of the most successful wineries in the country. Her dad expanded the business and grew the family wealth. We were introduced by my college roommate who is friends with her family. At first, it was great. She is an athlete and we seemed to share a great deal in common. But when we moved up here to Boston, something seemed to change in her. Her ambition suddenly seemed much more important to her than our relationship. All of a sudden, nothing I did seemed good enough. Even though I am a partner in a well-known law firm, that is not good enough and my salary is not good enough and my friends are not good enough. So, for that and other reasons, we have grown more distant the last couple of months, and she has taken to talking to me by text as she is often out of the house before I wake up, or home after I am asleep."

Patricia suddenly felt somewhat angry. "Tom, while I do appreciate your honesty and openness, I don't understand *why* you are telling me all of this. That is *very* personal information. Is that why you wanted me to come out here to talk?"

"Oh, my gosh. No." Answered Harris as he realized he had said *way* too much. "I am so sorry. I actually have no idea why I just unloaded all of that personal dreck on you like that. It just came out and I am truly sorry. I had no plans to tell you – or anyone – about any of that. I promise you. It just came out."

Patricia started to put her things back into her green cooler. "So, what did you want to talk to me about then?"

Harris now seemed honestly troubled with the fact that he had not only said too much, but because he had, just realized it had affected Patricia on a deeper level.

"The firm," he answered softly. "I truly only wanted to talk about the firm and let you know that myself and a few of the other partners and associates – most especially the ones who came with me – are sincerely bothered by the harsh treatment suffered by the legal secretaries and non-timekeepers at the firm and are planning to go to the capital partners to make our feelings and displeasure known."

Patricia stood up as her head was still swimming in a vortex of feelings. "That's very nice Tom and I am honestly happy to hear you say that. Hopefully, it will make a difference going forward. Now if you don't mind, I am going to take a quick walk before returning to the office. Thank you most kindly for asking me to lunch."

Tom was now at a loss at what to say or how to feel. "Of course. Of course…it's…ah…it's a great day to get some fresh air."

As she started to walk towards Beacon Street, Tom called out after her.

"Patricia. I truly am sorry for revealing so much of my personal issues and apologize if any of that hurt you in any way."

Patricia stopped and looked over her left shoulder at Harris. "Don't be silly. It did not hurt me at all. Why would it? Thank you again for listening and good luck with your issues…and…the firm."

As she turned to walk away, Harris watched her progress toward Beacon Street for a good thirty seconds. All the while shaking his head in anger at himself for saying too much about his relationship with his fiancé.

He knew a "Goodbye" when he heard it, and Ryan had just delivered an unequivocal "Goodbye" to him.

As Harris turned to walk back towards Tremont Street and the firm, he was shocked to realize the emotions *he* was now feeling.

Half-way back to Tremont Street, he sat on a bench near the Park Street "T" station and just stared blankly at the ground.

"What is wrong with you," he muttered to himself. He then switched from muttering out-loud to thinking frantically to himself. *I just met this woman. Why did I share so much personal information with her and why am I so bothered that I seem to have hurt her in some way? I don't feel remotely this bad after Simone and I have one of our never-ending arguments.*

After another couple of minutes of thinking and serious self-reflection, he suddenly jumped up off the bench with a huge smile on his face. He did so with so much enthusiasm and energy that he actually startled an elderly couple walking past.

"I am so sorry," he said as he waved at them and double-timed it back to his office.

Chapter Nine

Patricia swept into the offices of *Donovan, Miller & O'Reilly* as if a new woman. After walking away from Harris and the park bench, she strolled mindlessly along the streets of Beacon Hill for an hour trying to organize her thoughts and her feelings. Just in front of the *Fairmont Copley Plaza Hotel*, things clicked into place and her mind became made up.

By the time Patricia reached her cubicle and her desk, she was surer than ever that not only had she made the correct decision, but that she had to implement it immediately before second thoughts or the harsh realities of her life reared their ugly heads and caused her to change her mind.

Just as she was putting her green cooler in the right-side bottom drawer of her desk, Gerald Donovan stomped out of his corner office and looked down the hallway toward her.

When he spotted her, he raised his voice as he said, "Ms. Ryan. Could you please step into my office?"

Patricia looked down the hallway toward the head of the firm with a confused look on her face.

"NOW." Ordered Donovan as he turned on his heel and marched back into his office.

As he did, Susan Winstead—the longest serving legal secretary at the firm and a strikingly beautiful woman of fifty-two with short salt and pepper hair and deeply tanned skin—waved at Ryan from her side of the hallway.

"The Silver Skunk has been looking for you non-stop for the last fifteen minutes," whispered Winstead as she stared at Ryan with genuine concern.

"Why?" Asked Ryan as she turned hesitantly to walk toward Donovan's door.

"I am not sure," answered Winstead. "But I think it has something to do with Tom Harris."

"Tom," asked Ryan in a voice which at the very least, betrayed some kind of deep-seated feeling.

"Yes," continued the highly respected and very intuitive Winstead who acted more like a den-mother to the younger women at the firm than the ranking legal secretary that she was. "*Tom*. The door was closed but I could hear Donovan raising his voice and even shouting while Mr. Harris was in there."

Surprisingly, at first to Winstead, Patricia simply shrugged her shoulders, smiled, and then gave her a quick wink as she headed toward sure trouble in Donovan's office.

But as Patricia approached Donovan's door, the lightbulb went off over Winstead's head as she surmised that Ryan had already mentally crossed a much tougher threshold than the one she was about to step over. Winstead understood that

Ryan had finally reached the point of no return with the firm and was totally at peace with whatever was about to come.

Just as Patricia reached Donovan's door, she looked back down the hallway and saw her friend and firm mentor Winstead standing there looking at her with not only a smile on her face but giving her the "thumbs up" sign.

Ryan quickly smiled back and entered the law firm's ninth circle of Hell.

Five minutes after Patricia entered Donovan's office, the phone rang at the desk of Maureen Ennis. Mo looked down and saw Donovan's name appear. From past experience, she knew that he usually only called her for one reason. Because he had just fired someone and wanted her to supervise them cleaning out his or her desk, to confiscate their entry badge, and then escort them on their *walk-of-shame* out of the building.

"Good afternoon, Mr. Donovan."

"Ms. Ennis," said Donovan with no delay or pleasantries. "I need you to come to Patricia Ryan's cubicle right away."

Mo caught her breath as a cold sweat immediately appeared on her back. "W-w-why is that Mr. Donovan?"

"First, because I just told you so, Ms. Ennis. And second, because I just fired her and want her out of this building immediately."

Donovan then slammed down his phone.

Thirty seconds later, Ennis was still holding her phone to her head in the exact same position as when she picked it up.

She was desperately trying to think. Desperately trying to make some sense of the brief but surreal conversation she had just had. Desperately trying to figure out how to help and be there for the best friend she had ever had in life.

After another minute of being frozen in place, she very slowly started to nod her head, while just as slowly hanging up the phone. She then doubled-checked an extension she knew by heart and then snatched the phone back up and punched in the four-digit number.

Chapter Ten

As Patricia was gently placing the last of her personal possessions into an *Iron Mountain* file box, she noticed a shadow fall across her desk. She looked up to see the stern looking face of Maureen Ennis staring down at her.

"Hi, PR." Said Ennis in a very disconnected voice. "I really hate to do this, but you need to hurry up and collect your stuff and then get out of here."

"*What*?" Asked a clearly shocked and hurt Ryan. "What are you talking about?"

Ennis stepped closer and lowered her voice even more. "Look, Sweetie. It is what it is. Donovan called me and told me he fired you and that I needed to get you out of the building right away."

"You *can't* be serious, Mo. My best friend is putting her Human Resources duties before me and our friendship."

Ennis nodded her head. "I have a job to do for the firm and the ugly part of it is escorting terminated employees out of the building."

"Is that what I am to you now? A *terminated employee*."

"Mr. Donovan is the chairman of this firm, and as long as I am an employee here, I have a duty to follow his orders."

Just then, a short, thin, and very wimpish looking man best described as a weasel in human clothing rounded the corner closest to Ryan and Ennis at top speed and slid on the carpet as he tried in vain to come to a complete stop.

The human weasel adjusted his black horn-rimmed glasses and moved his overly long, stringy, and greasy brown hair back into place as he tried to look important.

The weasel's name was Michael Crowley. Two years earlier, he had become the youngest partner in firm history purely on his ability to kiss Gerald Donovan's butt as often as needed to both shield his complete incompetence and inexperience as well as keep himself on the promotion and bonus train.

He brought in little or no business to the firm, but with Donovan's help, attached himself like a leech to the clients and matters brought in by others who actually had legal, business, and marketing skills. With that as his only path to success, puckering up occupied the majority of his work days. So much so, that a few of the more courageous assistants anonymously left a box of *ChapStick* on his desk two years earlier as a prank birthday present.

Included in his duties as "Chief-Butt-Kisser" in the firm, was to act as the henchman and enforcer for Donovan. Crowley excelled at this task simply because he enjoyed inflicting pain and hardship upon those more talented than himself. Which at last count, was everyone at *Donovan, O'Reilly, & Miller.*

Crowley looked at Ryan with a twisted grin of pleasure upon his pinched and pasty-white face.

"I need to have your building access badge now, Ms. Ryan."

Patricia frowned up at the slight and self-important creature before her. "Why are *you* here asking for that? That's Maureen's job as the *head* of Human Resources," finished Ryan as she nodded toward her friend.

The weasel snapped his fingers and held out his right hand as he looked over at Ennis and then back down at Ryan.

"Not any more it isn't. Ms. Ennis was just fired for gross insubordination. She called Mr. Donovan on the phone a few minutes ago and said some truly obscene and disgusting things to him."

Patricia then shifted her eyes from the rodent to her best friend who now had a huge smile on her face.

"You can take the girl out of Dorchester, but you can't take the *Dorchester* out of the girl." Said Ennis in triumph.

"Whatever, white trash." Said Donovan's main bootlicker. "Just hand over your badge as well and then get out."

Instead of answering, Maureen bent down over the edge of Ryan's cubicle, picked up the half-full glass of water sitting next to the phone, and threw the contents in the weasel's face.

"Vermin like you are not allowed to call *anyone* white trash. If you *ever* reach that level, it will be a promotion, you troll."

With that, she unclipped her badge from her waist and threw it at the feet of Crowley.

Ryan then unclipped her badge and placed it neatly on her desk. She then stood and picked up her box of belongings. As soon as she did, she noticed that Ennis had her own box loaded up on a little hand cart.

"Hey, PR." Said Mo. "Just put your box on top of mine."

Ryan did and then embraced her best friend in the hardest hug she had ever given anyone.

"I love you, Mo." Whispered Ryan.

"I love you too, Sweetie."

As they separated from their embrace, Crowley – who was still patting his now *wet* stringy hair into place—pointed to the little hand cart. "*That* is firm property. That stays here. You can *carry* your boxes of junk out of the building."

Mo pretended to leap at Crowley, and he immediately cowered and almost fell into the fetal position.

"We are taking the cart with us, Rodent. If you want to stop us, *man-up* and take your best shot. If not, get out of the way."

Crowley looked in the eyes of Ennis and what he saw activated his survival instinct. He quickly stepped out of the way.

Chapter Eleven

Twenty minutes later, Patricia and Mo were seated at a table for two at the *Oak Long Bar & Kitchen* within the grounds of the always elegant and refined *Fairmont Copley Plaza Hotel* which was a bit of kismet as Patricia had mentally set her life changing decision in cement just as she crossed in front of the world-famous property not much more than an hour earlier.

Mo had guided both to the hotel because for years, Patricia was always mentioning that it was "the best and most beautiful hotel in Boston with its two majestic lions guarding the front entrance. And that since it had opened its doors in 1912, it had only gotten better."

Knowing she loved it but also knowing Patricia was on a very tight budget, Mo decided it was going to be her treat as a way to try and lift the spirits of her friend.

After the server placed a white wine in front of Patricia and a Sam Adams beer in front of Mo and then left to attend another table, Mo picked up her glass of beer, and looked at her friend who until recently—with the burdens of life now crushing her—had always managed to look classy and composed in public no matter the circumstances.

"Cheers, girlfriend." Said Mo. "As of today, we are both footloose and fancy free…and most likely homeless within four months."

Patricia laughed and clinked her glass to Mo's.

After Patricia took a small sip of her wine and Mo a large sip of her beer, Mo looked across the table at her friend whose dark eyes were framing the sunlight being reflected off the windshields of passing cars outside of the window of the restaurant.

"Okay, sister. You first. Spill it. What happened?"

"Gee, I don't know really," said Patricia with a smile. "It's been a whirlwind of activity and emotions since lunch time."

Mo perked up now. "I bet. Speaking of lunch time, let's start with the best part. How did it go with Hollywood Harris?"

"*Hollywood*?" Asked Patricia.

"Yes," smiled Mo. "That's what some of the other legal secretaries began calling him as he looks like he should be working up on the silver screen in Hollywood instead of a stuck-up law firm in Boston."

"Interesting. I had a similar thought regarding Tom and Hollywood." said Patricia as she delicately placed her glass down upon a small blue and white napkin on the table. "Anyway, it went very well with '*Hollywood Harris*. Right up until the moment he mentioned he had a *fiancé*."

"Ouch." Answered Mo.

"Yes. Quite right. And not just *any* fiancé, but that woman Simone who is the weekend anchor for Channel 5."

Mo let out a whistle. "Wow. I've seen her. She puts *Victoria Secret* models to shame."

"Thanks," said Patricia as she cast her eyes downward.

"Oh, not to worry, Sweetie. You've got her beat across the board. Besides, while she's undeniably beautiful, she comes across as cold and calculating. At least on television."

"I don't even know why I care. I don't really know the man other than a few short conversations at work and todays at the park."

"Oh, give me a break," answered Mo. "You light up every time you talk about him and from what you said, it seems he is quite impressed with you as well."

"It seems not. I am not going to pretend I don't find him attractive. I most certainly do. But what really appealed to me was that he truly seemed a step above the other partners and lawyers in the firm and at least on that count, I believe I was correct. *Despite* his fiancé."

"What makes you say that?" Asked Mo as she noticed the sidewalks starting to fill up with the first wave of workers heading home.

"It was because of Tom that Mr. Donovan called me into his office. Apparently right after our very informal lunch on the park bench, Tom walked into Mr. Donovan's office to tell him that he believed the legal secretaries and non-timekeepers were being treated unfairly. Tom never mentioned a word about me."

"That makes no sense. Then why did the Silver Skunk call *you* on the carpet?"

Patricia let out a small laugh as she shook her head. "Well...it really does actually...and you won't believe this..."

"I'll believe anything about that wanna-be dictator," interrupted Ennis.

"...Okay, well then add this to your list of the things you believe about him. As you know, one set of the windows in his corner office face the Common. Well, it seems from way up on the 26th floor, Mr. Donovan spied Tom walking into the park. At that point, he picked up a pair of binoculars he keeps on the inside ledge of his window and proceeded to watch him all the way until he sat down next to...me."

"How do you know that?"

"Because," answered Patricia as she made a face of disgust. "He told me himself in-between the constant eruptions of spittle coming out of his mouth as he yelled at me."

Ennis nodded her head. "So naturally, he thinks you spilled the Boston-baked beans to Mr. Harris about the deplorable and clearly illegal work conditions at the firm."

"Naturally. After he stopped to take a breath and wipe his chin, I told him that I had said nothing to Tom. Fortunately, because he was acting in such an unprofessional and boorish manner, it became quite easy for me to slip in that I intended to take a leave of absence from the firm."

"Let me guess." Smiled Ennis. "At that point, he said don't bother taking a leave of absence because you are fired."

"Precisely."

"So, now what?"

Patricia ran her fingers quickly through the front of her short black hair and then patted it back in place before answering.

"Now," answered Ryan with her biggest smile of the day. "It's *Operation Audrey Hepburn*."

"You still can't be serious about *that*."

"More serious than ever. And if you come by our place tonight for dinner with mom and Nana, I will fill you in on more of the details."

Mo shook her head in honest worry. "This is crazy beyond words. You know that, right?"

Patricia pursed her lips and nodded in reply. "I know. I really do. But I truly feel that if I don't embark on this crazy and clearly foolish journey, I will literally go insane from the stress and the sadness of it all. It's the oddest feeling. For some reason I can't explain, I feel like this trip and this fantasy, will save me, or at least give my mind a much-needed break."

"Okay," answered her best friend. "I don't entirely understand what you are feeling or what's going on inside that incredibly beautiful head of yours, but I do support you. And always will."

Patricia's eyes once again became tinged with tears as she reached across the table to hold Mo's hand. "Thank you so very much. I only wish you would reconsider and go with me."

Maureen squeezed her friend's hand tightly in response. "PR. I get that you are not thinking quite clearly right now, but do you honestly believe I just got myself *fired* in support of you if it was my intention *not* to go with you?"

"You're going?" Asked Patricia in a tone of voice associated with finding a dream present under the Christmas tree.

"Try and stop me." Laughed Ennis. "Besides. Someone is going to have to record this misadventure of a lifetime."

Chapter Twelve

After getting her mother and grandmother off to sleep by about 9:30 PM, Patricia walked into the living room carrying a silver tray holding two coffee cups, a small silver coffee pot, a ceramic creamer and sugar set, two linen napkins and two small spoons.

"Oh," exclaimed Mo when she saw the tray being placed upon the coffee table. "No coffee for me. Remember. I can't handle caffeine anymore after 3 PM."

Patricia laughed at her friend's response. "What's the problem? It's not like you have to get up for work in the morning."

Ennis joined Ryan in laughing which they proceeded to do for the next thirty seconds or so with genuine laughter trailing off to nervous laughter with the reminder of *why* they could sleep in if they chose.

"Besides," said Patricia as she cleared her throat. "It's decaf."

With that, Mo looked suspiciously at the pot as Patricia began to pour her a cup.

"Is this that *Paul's* coffee again or whatever from Seattle?"

"It's *Peet's*, and yes, it is. Just try it please. You liked the regular version. Give this one a chance."

"Heaven help me if we really do go to Paris. I'm terrified with the thought of the things you will force me to try."

After pouring her own cup and adding just a touch of half & half and one lump of sugar, Patricia looked over at Mo and smiled.

"Other than escargot and a bunch of cheeses you have never heard of, I think you will be safe. Now, speaking of Paris, I came up with a plan and an itinerary which will work and more importantly, fit my budget."

Mo clattered her small spoon back and forth off the inside of her coffee cup as she stirred in her cream and sugar. "*Your* budget? What about *my* budget? I'm going on this extravaganza as well you know and I'm counting pennies just like you."

"Not to worry," cooed Ryan. "I've got us covered. Besides, you make more money than me, so you don't have to worry about the pennies."

Mo shook her head emphatically with her long blonde hair covering most of her face until she cleared it.

"*Made.* As in the past. Besides, you know I just put the deposit down for that cabin on the Cape for Labor Day, so the *only* thing in my bank account at the moment is cobwebs. And as for you covering me. Forget it. You know I don't travel that way. Cape Cod cabin or not, I should have *just* enough if you don't go all crazy on me and rent a private jet for us."

"Shoot." Smiled Ryan. "How about just a Lear 35 so we can use up our entire budget on one flight."

"Okay. That sounds reasonable. Now tell me what wicked-cool plan you have cooked up for us?"

Ryan started to answer then unexpectedly shook her head and stopped. Nervously taking a sip of coffee instead.

"What?" Asked Mo. "You were just bursting to tell me your plan *one* second ago. Now, you are going to clam-up on me?"

Patricia nodded her head in the affirmative.

"Okay, so what. We are back in the first grade, and you are too shy to talk now?"

Patricia nodded her head again.

"Because you just chickened out and are once again rightfully afraid I am going to laugh in your face."

Patricia smiled and bobbed her head up and down.

"Well, I'm either going to laugh or cry or maybe both, so you might as well tell me."

Patricia smiled at her friend and then finally spoke.

"Okay, I will. But at least don't cry. I don't think I can handle you crying at the moment. I'm doing enough for both of us."

"Fine. I'll save that until I'm home in bed curled up with my Teddy Bear."

"Hopefully," said Ryan as she looked down and brushed some imaginary lint off her blue skirt. "That won't be necessary."

When she looked back up, she had some of the rekindled spark of fire in her eyes.

"I've been doing a good deal of research the last few nights and in a nutshell, here is what I have come up with. We head down to New York City and do something related to Tiffany's. From there, we head off to Paris for our museum outing, and then from there, we are off to Rome for our version of a *Roman Holiday*."

"*That's* it? That's your great thought-out plan? Sounds like there are an awful lot of holes there, *Audrey*."

"Actually," smiled Patricia. "There are none. I have figured out almost everything, including modes of transportation, places to stay, and our complete schedule. I will have the rest figured out by tomorrow morning."

"Well," laughed Ennis. "You *at least* have to count the holes in our heads for embarking on this fantasy of yours."

"Point taken." Answered Patricia. "Other than the holes in our heads, we are basically good to go."

"I doubt it, but let our adventure begin."

Chapter Thirteen

For Patricia, the toughest part of her plan and the entire journey to come, was just about to begin. She had to tell her mother and grandmother that she was going to leave them for possibly an undetermined amount of time.

As she finished washing the breakfast dishes, her mom and grandmother sat at the kitchen table whispering back and forth to each other and giggling.

Patricia turned around and smiled at them as she dried her hands on the dish towel. *Oh, how I do love them*, she thought.

For her entire life, they had been the two most loving, caring, decent, and protective people she had ever known. During her childhood and teen years, they sacrificed everything to make her as comfortable and as happy as possible. Now, it was *her* turn.

The fact that they were both still mostly blissfully ignorant to the darker side of people and the world, made them all the more precious to her. Because of them, she still believed that goodness, hope and even faith were more than just hollow words to be used as punchlines in jokes. Because of them, she still looked for the silver-lining in the blackest of clouds. Because of them, still tried to focus on the light at the end of the darkest of tunnels. And because of them, she still believed tomorrow could be better than today.

No matter how much pain they were in, no matter how difficult it was for them to do life's basic tasks, and no matter how many trips they had to make to the doctor's office or the hospital, they never stopped smiling, never stopped seeing the goodness in people and never lost faith.

They did not, but Patricia's faith in everything was being shaken to its very core. For her, it was now or never to break at least momentarily free of the shackles of real-life and experience at least a sliver of adventure – and maybe even true happiness – for herself.

"Mom. Nana," began Patricia. "I need to speak with you for a few minutes about something very important."

Her mom and grandmother looked at each other and began giggling again. The more Patricia frowned at them in confusion, the more they giggled like two schoolgirls back in the playground.

When they stopped, Patricia's mom looked up at her from the kitchen table. "When are you leaving, Sweetheart?"

"When am I…*what*?"

"When are you leaving on your *Audrey Hepburn* world adventure?"

"How?" Said Patricia. "I don't understand how…"

Her seventy-six-year-old grandmother Virginia, moved her white hair out from in front of her eyes and spoke for both of them. "The walls in this apartment are not exactly soundproof, Patty."

Patricia smiled down at the *only* person she allowed to call her "Patty" and then leaned down to give both a hug.

She then pulled up a chair at the table and joined them.

"So. How much do you know Mom? Or at least, how much do you *think* you know?"

Her mother winced in pain as she leaned forward to take her daughter's hands in hers. "I know – and we know – enough to know that you desperately need a break. You need a break from that awful law firm, and you even need a break from two old women who are stifling your life and robbing you of your chance to meet a nice young man and blossom fully into the beautiful and intelligent woman you are."

"Mom," pleaded Patricia with hurt, shock, and even shame radiating from her eyes. "Please don't ever say or even *think* that again. You and Nana are *everything* to me. You are my life."

"That's the problem, dear." Said her grandmother. "We've become *too much* of your life. We've become a burden and we are sorry."

"Nana. Stop." Said Patricia in a louder voice. "You've never been a burden. You and mom are my joy on earth. I am blessed to have you as my grandmother and mother."

"Be that as it may," said her grandmother as she leaned over to place her hands on top of those of her daughter's and Patricia's. "It's time for the baby bird to leave the nest and strike out on her own...at least for a little while."

Patricia slowly and gently pulled her hands from under the grasp of her mom and grandmother as nervous energy had her walking back to the kitchen sink to look out the window and gather her thoughts.

As she did, the one thought which repeated over and over was: *They really want me to go. How truly blessed I am to have these women as my role models.*

"Okay," she said firmly as she turned back from the window to look at her smiling mom and grandmother. "Your little eavesdropping ears have served you both quite well. Congratulations."

Patricia then laughed as she sat back down. "In the miniscule chance you did not quite hear everything correctly, let me fill you in on the entire plan as I now have it."

Both her mom and grandmother sat up straighter in excitement with the dual thoughts that first, the person they loved more than life itself, was thankfully taking a much needed leap of faith and discovery, and secondly, that they could at least live part of her journey vicariously.

Ten minutes later, Patricia finished giving her report. At least as much as she had planned.

"Wow, Sweetheart." Said her mom. "That's amazing and sounds like a movie all by itself. I'm very touched that all of this sort of sprang from that very special moment we shared when we watched Audrey Hepburn in *How to Steal a Million*" all those years ago.

Patricia reached over and took her mom's hand again.

"Yes. *Audrey* got us through quite a few depressing moments over the years and if I am going to honor anyone with this crazy stunt of mine, it's going to be you, via…her.

Besides, what the worst that can happen? At the very least, I get some nice photos of myself and Mo at some of the places she walked and worked. I can settle for that."

"You're going to have a magical time, dear." Said her grandmother. "No need to worry about us at all."

"Well, actually," stressed Patricia as she looked from one to the other. "I'm going to be a little less worried because Cousin Janice and her husband David have agreed to come over and check on you both from time to time as well as keep you company. They live just a few minutes away in Dedham and I'm also going to leave their cell and work numbers up on the refrigerator. They said you can call them any time day or night."

"That won't be necessary." Said her mom. "But it will still be nice to have them visit while you and Maureen are on your much needed adventure of a lifetime."

Chapter Fourteen

After speaking with her mom and grandmother, Patricia still felt somewhat guilty. Not only did they support her unequivocally, but even in their pain and constant discomfort, were in much better spirits than her.

Since she had been a little girl, her mom and grandmother had inspired her, and it was no different now. *I have no right to feel sorry for myself with them as examples*, thought Patricia. Time to try and snap out of it.

Carrying a Manila folder and with a newfound spring in her step, Patricia practically skipped the four blocks to Mo's two-bedroom apartment at 16 Hamilton Street.

Her mission now was twofold. First, fill-in Maureen on the rest of the itinerary and agenda as possible. And second and more importantly, help her pack.

Wearing cream-colored shorts, a royal blue Polo-shirt, and blue walking shoes trimmed in white, she bounded up the front stairs of Mo's apartment two at a time.

After ringing the bell twice with no answer, Patricia took out her iPhone and called Mo.

Five seconds later, she was greeted with a shouted "WHAT?" over the phone.

"Hi, Mo," laughed Patricia. "It's me. I'm at your front door."

"Why didn't you ring the bell?"

"I did…twice."

"Oh."

A few seconds later, Mo opened the door. She was still wearing her New England Patriots robe with her hair going in about a hundred directions.

Patricia looked at her and smiled. "Are you alright?"

Mo waved at herself with her right hand. "What do you think? We are leaving tomorrow for this escapade of yours – which I happily agreed to – and I still don't really have a clue what's going on or what to pack."

Patricia stepped in and closed the door behind her. "Not a problem. Answers and help have arrived."

Mo starred at her for a moment before finally answering with the beginning of a smile. "Oh, really? And here I was thinking I had something to worry about."

With Mo now dressed in a white warm-up suit adorned with Boston Red Sox logos on the jacket and pants and her hair now in place, she sat with Patricia at her kitchen table, and she watched her best friend hesitantly open her folder.

"Okay," said Patricia as she took a sip from her glass of ice water. "Before I begin, I want you to promise me there will be no arguing over the itinerary, hotels, travel, or anything."

Mo looked at her and shook her head. "What? Is this a dictatorship now?"

"No...well...maybe...*yes*...I think it is. At least a *benevolent* dictatorship. It means the world to me that you are going on this trip with me. More than I can ever tell you."

"It's my pleasure...and my place. I couldn't and wouldn't do anything else. You know that."

Patricia reached over and held Mo's hand. "Don't make me cry again. I am trying to break that newfound habit."

"Okay. But thanking me is not something I was going to argue about." Smiled Mo.

"I know," nodded Patricia. "It's what comes next."

"And what's that?"

Ryan shook her head. "Before I continue, you have to promise no arguing about anything."

It was Mo's turn to shake her head. "That ain't gonna happen, Sweetheart. I say 'yes' and next thing I know, you have enrolled me in some art school in Rome or some five-star cooking class in Paris."

Patricia laughed. "Well, those are both actually *very* good suggestions that we can follow-up on later, but nothing to worry about now."

"Great. So can we just end the mystery and get on with it?"

Patricia became very anxious as her dark eyes suddenly took in everything in the kitchen except her best friend.

"Well," she began. "There is only *one* thing you can't argue with me about."

"Are you going to tell me before it's actually time for us to leave?"

Patricia let out a deep breath and then blurted out her one condition. "I am paying for our travel and hotels and that's it. No arguing."

Maureen burst out laughing as she crossed her arms.

"No, really." She said after she stopped laughing. "What's your big mysterious condition?"

"That's it," answered Patricia without a trace of a smile on her face. "I am picking up the cost of our travel."

Mo looked at her friend and realized she was serious. "Not if you want me to come along, you're not."

"Mo. Please." Begged Ryan. "I am barely hanging on by my fingernails, here. I just got fired. I am responsible for getting you fired. I have no idea what's *really* in store for us during this trip, or most especially, afterwards. I have lost control over everything in my life. Including and most especially my *life*..."

Patricia took another long sip of water before continuing. "...As you said, this trip will most likely be a disaster. That's how it is in real life. In a movie, there is usually a happy ending. In real life, the vast majority of the people on the planet live in misery with zero prospects for a better life. I live in the real world. There's a better than even chance my life may actually get *worse* because of this crazy trip, but my mind needs it more than anything right now. As we talked about, I don't have a rational explanation for that. None. It's a silly thought and an even sillier plan that at least makes me happy for the moment and creates a ray of hope. No matter how faint it may be. So even if you were not the *best* best friend of all time and agreed to go on this escapade, I was still going to go and therefore would still have to foot the bill. So, in reality, all you would be doing would be sharing rooms and modes of transportation I was going to have to pay for on my own anyway."

Mo knew Patricia since they were both little girls and knew this was no time to argue with her friend. When the time did come, Mo had every intention of paying for at least half the trip, but now was not the moment to wage that particular battle.

Mo looked at Patricia and smiled. "Okay. But now you have to agree to one condition of mine."

"What's that?"

"That as a way of maintaining a modicum of my pride and not making me feel like a complete mooch, you at least allow me to pay for the meals along the way."

Mo watched as her friend did some mental calculations in her head.

"Done." Smiled Patricia as she let out a laugh of relief.

"Wicked cool," answered Mo in Boston slang. "Now, can you tell me what you have in the folder of yours and what the heck the plan is?"

Chapter Fifteen

"Okay." Said Patricia. "Well, with regard to the travel, first some good news. You know Cheryl McKenna at the firm?"

"Sure. She heads up the hotel practice."

"Exactly. Well, aside from being a partner, she's an amazingly good person. She called me last night at home to check on me – and us – and asked if there was anything at all she could do."

Mo smiled as she started to see this one parading down 5th Avenue. "And did you have a brainstorm?"

"I did." Giggled Ryan. "With my mental frame of mind being what it is as well as my newfound freedom from the firm, I decided to throw caution to the wind and take her up on her offer and ask for a favor."

Mo smiled. "Wow. That's a big step for you."

Patricia smiled back. "Tell me about it. Anyway, I mentioned that you and I were going on a little field trip with a few hotels included, and Cheryl immediately volunteered to see if she could get us some discounts that would make it much more affordable for me and my budget."

"And did she?"

Patricia whistled. "I'll say. She just called before I came over and she was awesome. Thanks to her…and it's a good thing you are sitting down for this…we are staying…are you ready…at the *Plaza* in New York City, the *St. Pancras Hotel* in London, *the Ritz* in Paris, and the *Intercontinental De La Ville* near the Spanish Steps in Rome."

"No way," yelled Mo with the news.

"It's true. But keep in mind, in each place, we are staying in their most basic rooms."

"Are you kidding me," said Mo in an excited voice. "The 'most basic room' in those hotels is better than anything I will ever *live in* during my entire life. Holy cow! This is awesome."

"Well," answered Patricia. "It makes me feel a little guilty to even say it out loud, but not only do we really need it, but I think we deserve a little First-Class treatment for the first time in our lives. Let's live like the upper crust for at least a few weeks."

"No one deserves it more than you, Sweetie."

Patricia blushed as she took out a sheet of paper from the folder.

"Thank you. Okay. Here is the report you have been waiting for. At least for this, the planets seemed to have aligned for us, as I was somehow able to put this together over the last several days and nights – with a huge assist from Cheryl this morning – without a problem. So…we leave tomorrow morning at 9:00 AM out of South Station on Amtrak to New York City. From there, we spend one night – and I still can't believe I am saying all this – at the incredible *Plaza*. The next morning at 6:00 AM commences '*Operation: Breakfast at Tiffany's*.' Later that afternoon…and here comes my big surprise…we board *The Queen Mary 2* for a seven-night Transatlantic crossing over to Southampton, England. From there, it's a two-hour motor-coach ride to the fabulous *St. Pancras Hotel* in London."

Patricia stopped in her presentation to take a look at Mo to see her reaction. She was not disappointed.

Her friend was sitting there with her mouth open trying to think of something to say.

"You have got to be kidding me…The Queen…We are taking that…when you talked about luxury, I knew your taste, but this is beyond *anything* I had imagined."

Patricia nodded as she pulled a different sheet of paper out of the folder with the printed *Queen Mary 2* information.

"Trust me," smiled Ryan. "It's surreal to me that I am even saying these things or having this conversation with you. I worked slave hours for this money so we might as well enjoy it. Once the trip is over, I will worry about real life and paying the bills then."

Mo started to say something, but then stopped herself not wishing to dampen the mood.

Patricia then continued. "We are staying in cabin 6288. It's an interior cabin, but from everything I have seen on-line and read about, the interior cabins on *The Queen Mary 2* are better than most cabins on other ships."

"Seriously," laughed Mo. "I'll stay in the engine room and shovel coal for a ride on *that* ship."

"Well." Answered Patricia. "Two things. First, it's technically not a 'ship.' *The Queen Mary 2* is an ocean liner. The best, the biggest, and the most elegant ocean liner in the world. It's the flagship of the *Cunard Line* which is the most historic and classy fleet on the ocean. Second, I think you have seen '*Titanic*' one too many times. No coal anywhere to be seen. Only state of the art technology complimenting the highest level of luxury."

"*Wow*, about the ship. And I know, about '*Titanic*.' Maybe I have seen it a few too many times."

"Well, speaking of that movie, I read that we will be sailing basically right over the spot where The Titanic sank and that people still throw flowers over the spot on the water. That said, I am *not* going to play Leonardo DiCaprio to your Kate Winslet and hold your arms up at the bow of the ship."

Mo laughed and snapped her fingers. "Darn it. You do know me too well."

"Back to our schedule. Or '*Shed-ule*' as they say in England. We spend two nights in London and then it's off to Paris on the Eurostar. What's great about staying at the *St. Pancras Hotel* – aside from the fact that it's a Five-Star hotel situated in an incredible location for tourists – is that it is also connected to the St. Pancras rail station. As in, the rail station where the *Eurostar* leaves from on its journey to Paris."

"Cool." Smiled Mo. "So, we can just fall out of bed in our pajamas and jump on the train to Paris."

Patricia smiled back at her as she looked her friend up and down. "Well, *you* can. I may be dressed a little more appropriately. Something very *Givenchy*."

"That's okay," said Mo as she shrugged her shoulders. "Part of my job on this trip is to be the comic relief and I intend to do my job to its very fullest."

Patricia knew her friend was still trying to lighten the mood and make her feel better and loved her all the more for the effort and kindness.

"After we get off the *Eurostar* in Paris – with you still in your pajamas – it's off to the *Ritz Hotel* at the *Place Vendome* – in the very heart of Paris—for the beginning of *Operation: How to Steal a Million*. As I think I mentioned to you, not only was part of the movie filmed there at the hotel, but Audrey Hepburn and Peter O'Toole actually stayed there during the filming."

"That's great," answered Mo. "But isn't that one of the most expensive hotels in the world?"

"It is." Agreed Patricia. "But also, one of the finest...if not THE finest in the world. They just renovated the entire hotel and made it even more luxurious and classy...if that is even possible. Cheryl got us a great rate, but even if she hadn't, I was going to stay there because of its history with the movie and with Audrey Hepburn."

"You are the Maestro. I am but a string player in the back of the orchestra."

"Anything, but." Answered Patricia. "After Paris, it's off to Rome by train for *Operation: Roman Holiday*. As mentioned, we will be staying just a stone's throw from the Spanish Steps at the truly awesome *Intercontinental De La Ville*."

"The Spanish Steps. Weren't they in the movie we watched on the Common the other night?"

Patricia gave Mo a look one would normally reserve for a beloved little nephew or niece, who was still learning – and mixing up – the months of the year.

"Why, yes, Maureen." Smiled Ryan. "That was completely lost on me. Now – purely by coincidence – we are staying at a hotel near an ultra-famous tourist attraction in Rome, which played a critical role in the movie *Roman Holiday*. How great is *that*?"

"Really?" Laughed Mo. "*Sarcasm*? Directed at your best friend in life who has always had your back."

"Sorry." Answered Patricia. "It was only a little sarcasm directed with a *huge* portion of love."

"Fine. So, I haven't seen the movie one hundred times like *some* people I know."

"Touché," laughed Patricia. "Now, on to the next subject. Getting you packed."

"Okay." Said Mo. "*Now*, you can go all sophisticated on me and let me have it. I don't have a clue what to bring."

Three hours later, after a lot of "*but why do I have to pack that?*" questions from Mo, the job was done with one large suitcase and one carry on now sitting neatly in a corner of Mo's bedroom.

"Okay," said Patricia now standing next to Mo's front door. "Just to be on the safe side, I have the taxi picking us up at 7:30 AM at my place. Please get there by 6:30 or 6:45 at the latest so we can have breakfast with my mom and Nana. Do you think you will need help with your suitcases?"

Maureen shook her head. "Please. Give me a break. I think I can schlep the suitcases four blocks all by myself. If I need help, I will call a Sherpa guide from Tibet to lease me his pet Yak for an hour."

Patricia looked at her friend and smiled. "You have a very unique mind with a very unique sense of humor, Maureen Ennis."

"I know." Agreed Ennis. "It's how I cope. You watch Audrey Hepburn movies. I say things which make sense to no one but me, and yet, still amuse me. I am an audience of one."

"That you are. See you bright and early in the AM, funny girl."

Chapter Sixteen

At 7:15 AM the next morning, Patricia's cell phone rang as she was sitting with her mom, grandmother, and Mo at her kitchen table.

She looked down and saw the number. "It's the taxi company," she announced. Then into the phone, she said, "Hello. Yes, we are ready. Thank you."

She then hung up and looked around the table. "Well, this is it. The taxi will be here in a few minutes. I am so... nervous and worried."

Her mom reached over and took her hand. "Don't be. Please. No one deserves this trip and escape more than you. You are going to have the time of your life, so please just enjoy it. Stop being the mature and serious woman who looks after everyone and at least for this trip, let your inner-child out, relax, and have a great experience."

Mo started to softly applaud from across the table. "Thank you, Mom. I could not have said it better. It's time for the actual very cute duckling to blossom into the beautiful and stunning swan. Time to announce yourself to the world, Sweetie."

Patricia let out a deep breath and then nodded her head. "Alright. I will try my very best not to be so serious and to try and remind myself how to have a good time. Okay?"

"That's all we can ask, dear." Answered her grandmother.

Patricia then stood up. "Thank you, Nana. Okay, well we are going to say goodbye to you guys here in the kitchen."

"No, you are not, young lady." Said her grandmother as she and her daughter rose from the table ever so slowly. "We are walking you out to the front porch to give you a proper hug goodbye out there."

Patricia knew better than to argue with her grandmother at this point while also realizing it was very important for them to show that they were perfectly capable of getting around on their own. Even if they were not.

"Thank you, Nana. That will be wonderful."

"Great." Said Mo. "But before we head out, I need a bathroom break. That fancy coffee of yours is going through me like Niagara Falls during the rainy season."

"TMI," whispered Patricia.

"What's that mean, dear?" Asked her grandmother.

"Oh, sorry Nana. It means 'too much information.'"

Her grandmother and mother laughed as they watched Mo make a beeline toward the powder room.

"Mo, we will meet you on the front porch," said Patricia to the closing door.

Three minutes later, Mo joined the three of them out front. What greeted her was a deep scowl from Patricia and two amused and intrigued smiles from Patricia's mom and grandmother.

"*WHAT-DID-YOU-DO*?" Mouthed Patricia as she looked at Mo with laser-beam eyes.

"What did I do about what?" Asked Mo loudly as she finished tucking in her shirt.

"*That*," whispered Patricia. "Him."

Mo looked down the front stairs to see Tom Harris standing there smiling up at them next to a Royal Blue Cadillac SUV with white leather seats.

"Oh," laughed Mo. "That."

"Yes…*that*." Answered Patricia as her eyes went from Harris – looking quite handsome in his black kakis, yellow golf shirt, and dark brown top-siders—to her mom and grandmother, to Mo, and then back to Harris and his two-hundred-watt smile.

"Mr. Harris called me last night. He wanted my advice about something."

"What?" Whispered Patricia again as she began to feel uncomfortable and awkward with Harris standing down there at the bottom of the stairs looking up at them.

"Well," smiled Mo like the cat who just popped the canary into her mouth. "Among other things, he wanted to know the best way to meet with you to apologize about something. I told him, if he wanted to do that, he'd have to wait a few weeks as we were off at 7:30 this morning for parts unknown.

He then asked where you lived, so I told him. That was it and here he is. Interesting. Right?"

Patricia's mom spoke up. "Patricia. Are you going to introduce us to the nice young man down there or do you intend to keep him waiting there all day smiling up at you?"

"Oh, sorry, Mom."

She then walked down the ten steps to the sidewalk to greet Harris.

"Good morning, Tom," Patricia said quietly.

"Good morning, Patricia." Said Harris as his smile grew even larger.

"If I may ask, what are you doing here?"

"Well," answered Harris as he shrugged his shoulders. "I spoke with Maureen last night and she told me you were off on your trip this morning so I thought I would stop by and give you a ride to the airport."

Patricia turned to look up at Mo and scowled at her again.

"That's very nice of you, Tom. But first, we are going to South Station, and second, we have a taxi on the way."

Harris looked down at Patricia and marveled at how truly stunning she looked in the early morning sunshine.

"Actually. The taxi driver was waiting here when I pulled up. I told him his services would no longer be needed."

Patricia opened her eyes a little wider with that comment. "That poor man. He drove all the way here."

Harris touched Patricia on the shoulder. "Oh, I think he was very happy judging by the smile he had after I tipped him. He was even whistling as he drove off."

Patricia did some more quick mental calculations and then let out another deep breath.

"Well…thank you for the offer then. At this point, since you have neatly painted us into a corner, we will kindly accept it. Now if you don't mind, I would like to introduce you to my mother and grandmother."

Harris smiled down at her and bowed slightly. "It will be my honor to meet them."

Harris then escorted Patricia back up the stairs to the shade of the front porch.

"Mom. Nana." Said Patricia as she looked from them to Harris. "This is Tom Harris from my now, *former* firm. Mr. Harris it seems, is going to be giving us a ride to South Station."

Patricia's mom and grandmother looked at each other with a knowing smile. With Patricia's grandmother even letting out a quick giggle.

Harris bowed again as he shook the hand of each woman.

"How very nice of you to offer, Mr. Harris." Said Patricia's mom who shifted her eyes from Harris to Mo standing behind him, who gave her a big wink in return.

"It's my pleasure, Mrs. Ryan. Most especially considering the way your daughter was treated by certain people at my firm."

"What a gentleman." Added Patricia's grandmother.

"Yes," said Patricia as she looked at Harris who was already picking up two of their suitcases to bring to his SUV. "It appears so."

"It seems chivalry is not quite dead," said Mo with a twinkle in her eyes.

"Well," answered Patricia to the group. "No matter the state of chivalry, we are most grateful."

As Harris started to walk down the stairs, Patricia added, "Oh, and mom. While we are gone, you and Nana can watch the *fiancé* of Mr. Harris on TV. She is the weekend anchor for Channel Five. *Quite* a beautiful and accomplished woman."

Harris stopped and hesitated on the stairs for just a second, smiled to himself, and then continued taking the suitcases to the car.

Mo looked at the three-woman next to her on the porch. "Even *more* intriguing. Right?"

While Patricia and Mo were exchanging hugs and kisses with Patricia's mom and grandmother, Harris brought the last two suitcases to the SUV.

When they came down the stairs, Harris first opened the back driver's side door for Mo and held her hand as he escorted her in before closing the door after her. He next walked Patricia to the front passenger door, opened it for her, and then took her hand as she stepped up and into the seat. He then softly closed the door behind her.

Once he was back to his door, Harris looked up at the two smiling women standing on the porch.

"It was a true honor to meet you both. I hope we can visit again soon."

"That would be wonderful, Mr. Harris," said Patricia's mom. "We would really enjoy it."

As the SUV slowly pulled away from the curb, Patricia's grandmother took her daughter's arm to walk back inside.

"What a wonderful young man," she beamed as she slowly shuffled toward the front door.

Chapter Seventeen

As they started the thirty-minute drive to South Station, Mo leaned forward from the back seat to address Patricia and Tom.

"I'm just going to zone out for a bit and listen to my country music."

"That's nice, Mo." Answered Patricia.

"Yes," continued Maureen. "I'm going to listen to *Take it Like a Man* by Michelle Wright. It's an oldie but a Goodie. She's not only awesome, but Canadian, you know. Like your relatives from Nova Scotia."

"Thank you, Mo." Said Patricia with just a hint of annoyance in her voice.

"Oh, no problem." Smiled Mo. "I will have my headphones on and as you know, I like to listen to my music *loud*."

"Great, Mo."

Maureen leaned further forward and patted her friend on her left shoulder. “Oh, you bet. I mean, the music will be so loud in my ears, you two could be screaming at each other up there and I wouldn’t hear a thing. Not a thing.”

Harris laughed out loud as he changed lanes.

Patricia turned around and gave Mo a mock glare. “*Thank you*, Mo. You can sit back now and listen to Michelle Wright now…loudly.”

Mo leaned back in her seat, smiled, pressed “Play,” on her iPod Shuffle and then began humming to herself.

As Harris navigated the sparse early morning Boston traffic, he turned quickly to look at Patricia.

“The real reason I am here is because I wanted to apologize for now—*two* things. First, for showing up unannounced and unexpected like this. Second, I wanted to apologize again for my behavior the other day on the park bench. I really don’t know what possessed me to talk so much. I swear, my *only* intention was to speak with you about the firm and the mistreatment of the legal secretaries that I and those in my group have witnessed.”

Patricia turned to look at him and was immediately hit with the reflected sun bouncing off the gold watch on his wrist.

“That’s okay, Tom,” Began Patricia. “No need to…I’m sorry…is that a *real* gold Rolex watch on your wrist?”

Harris glanced at the watch and then a bit sheepishly over at Patricia.

“It is. But actually…”

"Oh, my apologies for prying. Except for in magazines, I've just never seen a real one before."

"Well," said Harris as he defensively dropped his left arm to his side to shield the watch from her view. "There is an interesting story which goes along with the watch..."

"No need to explain...nor...justify."

Harris laughed as he now brought his left hand back up to hold the steering wheel. "No justification at all being offered. Since you mentioned it, I just wanted to give you a bit more background about me...and the watch. Would that be okay?"

Patricia looked at Harris and smiled. Both at him and because of the confident tone of his voice. "Of course. Please continue."

"Thank you," nodded Harris as he stole a quick glance in the rearview mirror to see Mo's head bobbing up and down to the music in her ears. "While I have become fairly successful as a lawyer, like you, I grew up in very humble means. I grew up in a small town in Virginia. My dad was actually the custodian for the public high school I attended, and my mom was a lunch lady there..."

Patricia tried and failed to stifle a laugh. "I'm sorry about that. Your mom was a *lunch lady*?"

"Yeah...right?" Smiled Harris. "She was one of those women they make fun of in every high school-based movie and most Disney shows."

The smile on Patricia's face disappeared as fast as it appeared. "Well, I bet she was a very hard worker."

"She was," agreed Harris. "They both were. I had two older brothers and two younger sisters and they somehow managed to not only keep a roof over our heads and feed us on little more than minimum wage jobs but set aside some money for college for us as well."

Patricia smiled at that. "You should be very proud."

"I am beyond proud, actually. My dad worked six days a week and then always took on an extra job or two during the summer break. Once, when I was twelve, I asked him why he worked so hard with no vacations. He looked down at me and laughed and said, he always wanted a gold Rolex watch and was saving up for one. Of course, the truth was, he and my mom spent every dime they made taking care of us."

Patricia felt her eyes beginning to mist up a bit and turned her head more toward her window. "Well, you and your brothers and sisters are blessed."

"Yes," nodded Harris as his own eyes began to water. "We were. When my dad finally retired six years ago, I bought him a gold Rolex as a present and most especially as a way to say thank you for all of his love and sacrifice."

Patricia looked back at Harris and his watch. "How wonderful. And you bought one for yourself as well?"

Harris slowly shook his head. "No. We lost my dad two years ago in a car accident. This is the watch I bought him."

"Oh, Tom," answered Patricia as a tear now fell from her left eye. "I am so very sorry I brought it up and so very sorry for your loss."

Harris reached over with his right hand and touched the back of her left hand. "No need at all to apologize. Maybe I need to say I am sorry for springing that story on you like that, but I just can't seem to keep anything to myself when I am around you."

Patricia opened her knock-off black *Prada* purse in search of a tissue.

As she did, Harris pointed to the glove compartment. "I have a small box of tissues in there in case you need one…" He then laughed to try and break the tension. "…I know I do."

After they both patted their eyes for a few moments, Harris went back to the original subject.

"So…anyway," continued Harris with a smile. "Sorry for surprising you this morning with my taxi service and sorry for my opening up so much the other day in the Common… and now."

"Done. Now, if you will accept my apology for turning on the water-works non-stop around you, then I think we should create a moratorium on apologizing for a while."

Harris nodded as he slowed for a city bus suddenly changing lanes in front of him. "Done."

Patricia then looked at Harris both in a coy and curious way. "Well, speaking of our conversation on the bench, won't your *fiancé* be upset that you are giving us a ride?"

"Maybe," answered Harris as he narrowed his eyes. "I'm not sure."

"Why not?"

"Well, two reasons," said Harris as he went back to his natural smile. "First, because I didn't tell her…"

"Why not?" interrupted Patricia.

Harris shrugged his wide shoulders. "Truthfully…first, because she did not come home last night. And second, even if she had, I am not sure I would have told her."

"Why not?"

Harris smiled wider. "Do you realize that is the third time you asked 'Why not?' in a row?"

Patricia did not return the smile as she gave no ground. "Don't try to change the subject. Why not?"

"Well, '*Why not*' is actually part of the subject, but be that as it may, I am not quite sure why I wouldn't tell her. Deep inside, I feel like the major reason being I would be afraid she would forbid me to come, and I really wanted to see you one more time before you left."

"Why?" Asked Patricia softly.

"Nice to see you cut '*Why not*' by fifty percent." Laughed Harris.

When Patricia did not join in his humor, he quickly continued.

"I don't know really. I was asking myself that question non-stop as I was driving to your home this morning. I actually pulled over once with the intention of turning back but didn't."

"Why not?" Asked Patricia in an even lower voice.

Harris turned and smiled at her before returning his eyes to the road. "The only real and honest answer I could come up with was because I and my psyche are desperate to be around a decent, moral, and normal person. I think it's one of those things that are mostly unexplainable and unprovable. Like when you are walking down the street and see a stranger from the opposite sex, and even though you only lock eyes for a nano-second, that feeling washes over you immediately that if you could simply talk to the person, you know the two of you would click on some level."

Patricia looked down at her fingernails. "And you felt that way about me?"

Harris nodded vigorously. "I did. From the moment I met you in the kitchenette at the firm and you gave me that dollar. It was refreshing on a human level just to speak to an obviously decent and classy person and think that person could become a friend..."

Harris quickly turned his head to look at her. "...*Platonic*, of course."

Like the word "Fiancé" in the park, the word "Platonic" sounded like a cannon-shot at close range.

Suddenly blushing, Patricia looked up both relieved and surprised to see that they were already pulling up to South Station.

"Wow," she said not fully facing Harris as she could still feel the warmth in her face. "That was fast. Thank you so very much."

Harris put his SUV in park, looked over at Patricia, and noticed the reddening color of her beautiful face.

A face, he instantly realized, he was going to miss tremendously once she entered the station.

"Did I say something wrong...again?" Asked Harris with a smile he had to force.

"Don't be silly," answered Patricia as she opened her door. "*Platonic* quite accurately describes our...acquaintanceship. As we have known each other for such a short time and really barely spoken, I'm not even sure we can use the word 'friend.' But no matter what it is, *platonic* works just fine. Something you might want to stress to your fiancé if you ever tell her you were kind enough to give Mo and I a ride this morning."

With that, Patricia turned and exited the front seat. It was only then that she noticed that Mo was not only out of the SUV but was around back trying to get the luggage.

Harris saw what Mo was doing and dashed out of his front seat to open the hatch-back of the SUV.

"No, no, no." He said in a slightly raised voice with the forced smile back on his face. "Sir Walther Raleigh here. No way I let the two of you lift the suitcases out of the back."

Mo stepped aside and laughed as she waved at Harris to proceed.

"Thank goodness," she said. "I was bluffing the whole way with that move."

Mo then looked over at Patricia for a reaction and saw that she was deep in thought while also seemingly anxious to get moving.

Harris soon had the two large suitcases and two carry-on size suitcases on the sidewalk next to the SUV.

"Please allow me to bring these to the gate for you."

Patricia shook her head. "Thank you, but no. We can manage from here."

She then picked up her carry-on and put it sideways atop the larger suitcase, pulled out the handle on the larger suitcase and then demonstrated how easy it was to now roll both.

"See." She punctuated.

Harris knew better than to argue. Not only were her lips pressed together firmly, but there was a hint of both sadness and disappointment in her eyes.

Harris tried his best to smile. "You're right. Good job. I guess you will be able to manage just fine…without me."

He then leaned over and shook Maureen's hand.

"Have a great time, Mo. And please be safe."

Mo nodded her head and then stepped-in to hug Harris. "Oh, we will," she said out loud. Then very softly, she added, "Don't give up on PR."

After Mo stepped away, Tom turned to face Patricia who had her natural color back. "I know we agreed on a moratorium, but sorry again for everything. My head is a little mixed-up at the moment."

Patricia reached out to shake the hand of Harris who slowly reciprocated. "Thank you for everything, Tom. For caring about the plight of the legal secretaries at the firm, to talking to me about it, to the kindness you showed my mom and grandmother, and most especially, for taking the time to give us a ride this morning. We are both so very grateful."

Feeling both numb and confused by the range of emotions running through his mind and body, Harris was not sure which answer would be safest.

"You are most welcome. Have a wonderful time. Maybe when you get back, the three of us can have lunch or dinner and you can tell me about the trip."

Patricia looked at him for several seconds, shook her head almost imperceptivity, offered one last weak smile, and then turned on her heel and walked quickly into the station.

As she did, Mo offered Harris her biggest smile, nodded her head toward the departing Patricia, and then winked at Harris before turning and double-timing it to catch up with her best friend.

Chapter Eighteen

It wasn't until the train was past Providence that Patricia spoke more than two words.

"Thank you for this. My mind is still sound asleep."

Mo smiled down at her best friend as she finished putting a "To Go" cup of coffee on the tray table in front of Patricia and then lowered her own and placed her coffee and a cinnamon coffee-roll on its vibrating and slightly tilted gray surface.

She then plopped back into her seat of the gently swaying train.

"Well," said Mo as she began to add cream and sugar to her coffee. "It's not the fancy stuff you drink, but it's good, hot, and hits the spot."

Patricia answered Mo with a real smile. "I know. I think Amtrak is an awesome company and does a great job. Their employees have always been wonderful to me, and I especially love riding on their overnight trains in a sleeper. I only did it once, but it was incredible. Something very romantic and peaceful travelling that way. I only wish they could get more support from the federal government. My grandfather George always told me 'Great countries have great passenger rail systems,' and I truly agree with him…"

She then looked out the window. "…and if you are travelling in the Northeast, Amtrak is the *only* way to go."

Mo nodded her head as she bit into her cinnamon roll.

"Yes," she said before taking a sip of coffee. "It really is relaxing and beats the stress of airports."

Mo then smirked as she purposefully changed the subject.

"So," she began. "That really was a very touching story Tom told you about his watch and his dad. What a wonderful son."

Patricia turned to face her friend. "Why, you little devil. I thought you said you were going to have the *Michelle Wright* CD blaring in your ears."

Mo giggled again. "I was and I meant to. That was before I found out my battery was totally out of juice."

"And when was that?"

"When I pushed 'Play,'" smiled Maureen.

Patricia looked at Mo and wrinkled her forehead. "But I saw your head bobbing up and down to the music when I looked in the rearview mirror."

Mo took a long sip of coffee then looked at Patricia with a wide smile. "Can I help it if I memorized the music and was imagining how it would sound if my iPod was working."

Patricia playfully pushed her friend on the shoulder. "I can't believe you did that. So you heard *everything*?"

"Not everything," giggled Mo again. "The traffic was a little loud at times and you guys quite selfishly spoke very quietly. What was up with *that*?"

Patricia laughed at some of the tension left her body. "Well, anyway. To close that subject for now, *please*. He *is* a very nice man, he *does* have a fiancé, and in case your radar-like ears did not hear, he *does* consider me a *platonic* friend. So now, can we *only* focus on the incredible adventure we just started?"

"Absolutely. And as for Tom, no way he said 'platonic' as a way to cover up the fact he might be falling for you and didn't want to make you nervous again," smiled Mo as she fiddled with her coffee lid.

Chapter Nineteen

Patricia could not stop turning her head left and right as she and Mo followed their luggage – and the quite handsome and polite bellman who collected it—into the *Plaza*.

As she took it all in, her mind flashed for just a second to the movie "Home Alone 2" which was filmed all those years ago in this iconic hotel.

Like many things in their life – and like the vast majority of people on the planet who struggled to makes ends meet – Patricia and Mo had only seen this incredibly famous hotel in movies such as that or described between the pages of a good novel. To now, not only see it in person, but to be staying in it that very night, was not something either of them had imagined prior to a few days ago.

As they made their way to the front desk, Patricia was amazed to see that everywhere she looked seemed to be filled with not just the "beautiful" people of New York City, but the "beautiful" people of the world.

Mo noticed it right along with Patricia. "Holy cow. A few of these women are wearing at least two years of my salary around their necks."

"Your *former* salary," corrected Patricia with a smile. "And yes. At least that much. Toto, we are not in Kansas anymore."

There was a short line to check-in which moved very quickly. When Patricia and Mo made it to the front desk, they were greeted with a surprise.

"Ms. Ryan," smiled the petit red-headed receptionist. "I am pleased to inform you that you have been upgraded to a mini suite."

Mo and Patricia turned quickly to look at each other before Patricia looked back at the receptionist.

"That sounds so wonderful, but I am sure there has been a mistake."

The receptionist shook her head and smiled in return. "Oh, there has been no mistake. I believe a friend of yours from Boston who consults for our parent company made the arrangements..."

Patricia and Mo looked at the receptionist, then at each other, and then said at the exact same time: "Cheryl."

Five minutes after yet another incredibly good-looking bellman escorted them up to their suite and helped them with their luggage, Patricia and Mo were still sitting on the sofa staring in wonder at the room – or really, rooms – before them.

At the far end of the 700 plus square-foot suite, lay the most luxurious four-poster bed either of them had ever seen. Between the bedroom section and the living room they now occupied, was an incredible and quite large fireplace. Off to the side was a separate kitchen, a walk-in closet, and a bathroom most people could only dream of.

"Remind me," said Patricia as she looked over at the fireplace. "To buy Cheryl several gifts from London, Paris, and Rome."

Mo nodded almost absently mindedly while staring at the four-poster bed. "Way ahead of you on that one, Sweetie."

Chapter Twenty

Precisely at 5:45 AM the next morning, *Operation: Breakfast at Tiffany's* began.

Patricia stood in front of one of the window displays at *Tiffany's* on 5th Avenue wearing knock-offs of Audrey Hepburn's iconic outfit consisting of the black cocktail dress, the large pearl five-strand necklace, the black evening gloves up to her elbows, and the dark sunglasses.

In her left hand, she held a small coffee in a cardboard cup and in her right hand, a Danish.

A short distance away near the corner of 5th Avenue and 57th Street, Mo had her iPhone out and was recording the entire operation.

Patricia had no idea what to expect other than she wanted to be silly and re-live a movie moment of her favorite actress of all time.

In the movie, Audrey Hepburn gets to eat her Danish and drink her coffee in peace as she marvels at the jewels on display in front of her.

Patricia was not quite so lucky.

Knowing Mo was filming the recreation, Patricia took a small bite of the Danish and then looked over at Mo about thirty feet away and smiled.

As she did, a very low male voice behind her suddenly said: "You going to finish that roll?"

Startled, Patricia jumped back around to see what appeared to be a homeless man standing two feet from her staring at her and her Danish.

"I'm sorry," said Patricia as she looked at the rather large, imposing, but still somehow dignified man. "What did you say?"

The homeless man nodded at the Danish in her hand. "You going to eat all of that?"

Patricia looked at the Danish, back at the man, and then handed him the rest of her "breakfast."

Instead of moving on, the big man simply stood right next to her as he began eating the roll while never taking his eyes off her face.

As he did that, behind her, Patricia next heard: "You wanna buy a *Rolex* watch?"

Patricia twirled back around to see a much smaller man now standing on that side of her with an open briefcase full of fake watches.

"What? No," she said at the little man. "I don't want to buy a *Rolex*."

As she said that, she noticed Mo now laughing uncontrollably as she tried to hold the iPhone steady while she continued to film.

"Can I have a sip of your coffee?"

Patricia turned back to see the big homeless man nodding at her coffee.

"My...what?" Asked Patricia.

"Your coffee. Can I have a sip? I need something to wash down the Danish."

Patricia handed him the coffee.

"Okay," the other man said in her ear. "You don't want a *Rolex*. How about a *Cartier* or a *Patek Philippe*? Fifty dollars for either one."

Patricia now heard Mo howling with laughter.

"No," said Patricia to the little man with the briefcase. "Nothing, thank you."

"Good coffee," said the homeless man. "Except I prefer mine black."

"How about a *Hermes* scarf?" Asked the little man as he pulled a handful of knock-off scarves out of his dirty pants.

Patricia looked past the little man toward Mo and motioned her friend frantically with her hand to come over.

Mo walked over smiling. "Yes...*Holly Golightly*?"

Patricia shook her head and smiled back. "Let's go."

A few feet removed from the homeless man and the illegal street peddler, they were greeted by a very tall, broad-shouldered and impeccably dressed doorman for Tiffany's.

"Would you two ladies like to step into the store for a few minutes?"

Patricia looked back at the two men still hovering ten feet away and then back at the doorman.

"Yes, please. That would be wonderful." Answered Patricia.

The doorman then escorted them into one of the most famous and photographed stores in the world.

Once safely inside, he asked: "You ladies recreating that *Breakfast at Tiffany's* scene?"

"One of us is," smiled Mo as she nodded at her best friend.

The doorman – who had a very warm face for someone who clearly doubled as security for the store – nodded as he smiled down at both.

"Yeah. I thought so. We get that sometimes. More than you might think. A few ended up coming in here to escape."

"They did?" Asked Patricia as she began to feel a bit foolish.

"Oh, sure." Smiled the doorman. "I don't know what 5th Avenue was like in 1961 when they filmed *Breakfast at Tiffany's*, but it can be a little challenging out there sometimes now."

"Thank you so very much for letting us in," Said Patricia.

"You are most welcome," smiled the doorman. "You can stand right here. As you can see, they are just getting the store ready for business. Those guys out there should be gone in a few minutes. They really don't mean any harm. Times are just a bit harder these days, that's all."

"I know," smiled Patricia up at the kind doorman. "That is one of the reasons I was doing this little reenactment. To take my mind off some of those tough times."

The doorman nodded.

"You know, I've seen a number of women over the years – including top-flight models for commercials – dress up like Holly Golightly in front of Tiffany's. But I've never seen anyone come as close as you to the character. If I may, there is something about you which encompasses the look, class, and kindness of Audrey Hepburn."

"Thank you," said Mo with a huge smile as she patted the doorman on the arm. "That's what I've been trying to tell her."

Chapter Twenty-One

Neither Patricia nor Mo had ever been on a cruise before. As they were greeted by impressively uniformed staff upon boarding *The Queen Mary 2*, Patricia had no doubt they were starting at the very pinnacle of luxury cruising.

To begin with, as she had told Mo, the almost 1,200 foot-long, 236 foot-tall, 135 foot-wide, 148,000 tonnage flagship of the Cunard Line was technically not a cruise ship at all, but rather an *Ocean Liner*. Not only was it the largest and most prestigious Ocean liner on the high seas, but with its inch thicker coating of steel than a typical cruise ship and its highly reinforced hull, it was built precisely to take the worst pounding the oceans of the world had to offer while delivering an incredibly smooth ride.

As they made their way to their cabin on deck six, Patricia was beyond excited to put their carry-on bags away and go check-out the full-size planetarium, the 3D cinema, the

20,000 square-foot spa, the elegant ballroom, the two-story library, and the rest of the magnificent vessel they were about to sail across the Atlantic to Southampton, England.

Mo opened the door to cabin 6288 and they both broke out in huge smiles as they looked inside and entered. While it was an *interior* cabin, it was still incredibly elegant with more than enough room for them.

Each twin bed was covered in a gold comforter, with a soft-red colored throw pillow sitting in the middle near the headboard. Next to each bed, was a nightstand made of blonde teak wood with an elegant bedside lamp on the center of each.

Off to the side, in front of the twin bed on the left as you entered the cabin, was a small table and comfortable armchair. On the other side of the cabin, also made of blonde teak wood, was a perfect size desk, with four drawers and a chair. Above the desk was a 40-inch flat-screen television. And as you entered the cabin, the luxuriously appointed bathroom with a large shower was on one side, with four generous closets being on the other side.

Mo made a beeline for the bed on the left and plopped down on it.

"Dibs." She said with a smile as she continued to softly bounce up and down from her leap.

"It's all yours," laughed Patricia as she placed her carry-on upon the luggage cover on the bottom of her bed. "I have my own luxurious version."

For the next six days and seven nights, Patricia and Mo lived a fantasy trip they had only dreamed about before they stepped aboard the "QM2" as the ship was referred to by those who sailed her often.

From the five-star dining in the Britannia Restaurant, to the casual dining in the Horizon Court, to ballroom dancing in the Queen's Room with incredibly debonair and talented "dance hosts," to the Broadway style shows in the Royal Court Theatre, to the daily lectures from world renowned experts in their fields, to the elegant high-tea each day, to being pampered in the spa, or simply falling asleep on a deck chair in the warm sun while reading, Patricia knew that the "crossing" itself as it was called, was an ultimate vacation for anyone and something to be truly cherished.

Chapter Twenty-Two

The dream trip for Patricia and Mo continued unabated as they walked into the lobby of the Five-Star *St. Pancras Hotel* located on Euston Road in London.

On their last full day on the QM2, Patricia sat on a lounge chair on the promenade deck bathed in the late afternoon sun and read about the hotel they were about to – thanks once again to Cheryl McKenna – stay in for their two nights in London.

The hotel was a converted historic landmark of London. The Victorian masterpiece had originally opened in 1873 and was known then as *The Midland Grand Hotel.*

About 150 years later, the building was more magnificent than ever as it retained all of its Victorian splendor on the outside with contemporary looks and five-star service on the inside. Many visitors were especially captivated by what they called the "Mini-Big Ben" clock tower attached to one end of the massive hotel and residence.

After taking a very comfortable and very modern motor-coach bus from the dock of the Queen Mary 2 in Southampton to the *St. Pancras Hotel*, Patricia and Mo were met with yet another amazing surprise upon their check-in at the front desk.

"I am very pleased to inform you," said the very tall and smiling young man addressing them. "That you have been upgraded from one of our normal rooms to a *Chambers* Suite."

Mo looked at Patricia and then turned to look back at the young man as she leaned across the counter toward him.

"And just want exactly," she smiled back. "Is a *Chambers* Suite?"

The young man leaned toward Mo in return. "Well. We like to think of them as the most luxurious rooms and suites in all of London. Each suite exudes Victorian charm with incredibly high ceilings, massive windows, ornate moldings, a huge working fireplace, the finest furniture and beddings, and bathrooms which rival any you will find in Buckingham Palace."

Mo looked at Patricia as she raised her eyebrows in delight and then looked back at the receptionist and sarcastically asked: "That's it?"

The front desk clerk knew she was very impressed and kidding so he played right along.

"Well, yes, ma'am." He frowned. "Sorry that is the best we can do...oh...except for the fact that each suite also comes with complimentary and private access to the *Chambers Club* which serves breakfast, lunch, light dinner and snacks, personal butler service, free Wi-Fi, and Eurostar valet service. After that…yes…that's about it, I'm afraid."

As the clerk and Mo began to laugh together at their shared joke, Patricia began to silently cry as she turned her head from them.

Mo looked at her and knew instantly what was up.

"Hey," she said as she tapped Patricia on the shoulder. "I thought you said you were going to try and control that stuff from now on."

"I'm sorry," said the young clerk with a look of concern replacing his smile. "Is everything alright?"

Mo reached across the desk and patted his hand.

"Everything is great. It could not be better. In fact, it might be *too* good. My friend is a bit emotional at the moment because she has never been treated with so much kindness or experienced so much luxury and tends to wear her feelings on her sleeve lately."

Patricia turned back to face Mo and the clerk as she finished drying her eyes yet again.

"This is wonderful news," she declared with now a wide and genuine smile. "We can't thank you enough for your help and for the kindness."

The front desk clerk looked back at her with both a softness in his eyes as well as a good amount of understanding. "Yes, Miss. Here in London, like some other parts of the world, regular working people are sometime assigned stations in life or even looked down upon by those more often than not, *born* into money. It's nice once in a while, for truly good people who have worked and sacrificed all of their lives, to experience a real slice of luxury from time to time."

Mo let out a laugh to lighten the mood. "Boy, you can say that again."

The clerk continued to look at Patricia. "During your two days with us here at the *St. Pancras*, please know that we consider you family and will be available to you 24 hours a day should you need anything. Anything at all."

"The only thing we will need," said Mo. "Is someone to help us wipe the smiles off of our faces."

As Mo turned to follow the bellman who had suddenly appeared out of nowhere, Patricia reached over to shake the kind young clerk's hand.

"Thank you."

"It is a true honor and pleasure, Miss Ryan." Answered the wise young man.

After two days of exploring London by double-decker tour bus and foot, it was time to board the *Eurostar* train for the two hour and fifteen-minute journey under the English Channel to Paris.

Not only was the *St. Pancras Hotel* perfectly situated above the station where the *Eurostar* departed, but per their promise, Patricia and Mo were personally escorted to the station by a bellman from the hotel as he pulled their luggage on a small handcart.

For Patricia, no matter how the overall adventure ended, she already considered it a blessing and a *huge* success based simply upon the kindness of some of the people they had met along the way.

Such kindness, she thought, was the *true* ultimate luxury.

Chapter Twenty-Three

The normally cheerful and carefree Mo had a look of real concern in her eyes coupled with maybe a thin sheen of sweat on her forehead.

"I don't like tunnels." She proclaimed.

"Pardon me," asked Patricia as she continued to watch mostly excited Europeans board the ultra-speedy and famous train.

"I don't like tunnels," repeated Mo.

Patricia looked out the window. "Well, we are not in a tunnel yet. We are still in the station."

"Yeah," answered Maureen as she continued to stare out the window at nothing. "But this thing goes through a tunnel. A wicked long one that is also wicked deep under a whole bunch of water."

Patricia shrugged her shoulders.

"Yes. It's called the *English Channel* and we are only under it and in the tunnel for 20 minutes."

Mo turned from staring out the window, to look at her best friend.

"How do you know that?"

Patricia waved a brochure at her. "Because I can read, silly."

Mo looked down at the *Eurostar* brochure as Patricia started to read.

"Just 35 minutes or so after we leave the St. Pancras Station, we enter the Channel Tunnel – or *Chunnel*, as some Americans call it. At certain points on our quick trip, we will be travelling almost 200 miles per hour. Next..."

Mo held up a hand as her face seemed to be turning a light shade of green. "Stop, please. It's much better if I don't know anything. Nothing about speed. Nothing about how deep the tunnel is. In this case, ignorance truly will be bliss."

Patricia looked at her friend and smiled as she folded and put away the brochure. "Okay. No more reading. I think what you need for the next two hours is a good distraction."

Mo nodded her head vigorously. "That's for sure. What do you suggest?"

Patricia reached into her black *Prada* bag and pulled out two booklets of *Sudoku* games.

"Let's have a contest," Patricia said knowing Mo liked to compete in about any game. "To see who finishes their *Sudoku* puzzle first. We will each have the same booklet and work on the exact same puzzle. How does that sound?"

Mo looked a bit startled as the *Eurostar* began to move smoothly out of the St. Pancras Station in London on its way to Paris.

"Doesn't sound like much a distraction to me," said Mo as she turned her gaze from the window to look at her strikingly beautiful and incredibly loyal friend. "But I'll give anything a try at this point."

"Great," answered Patricia as she gave Mo her *Sudoku* booklet and handed her a small pencil. "Let's do the puzzle on page 32."

They both instantly started. As least Mo did. Patricia mostly just watched her friend with a bemused smile on her face as Mo focused on completing the puzzle while the tip of her tongue peeked out of the left side of her mouth from total concentration.

After this went on for a while, Patricia leaned over and tapped Mo on the shoulder.

"What?" Asked Mo still totally absorbed with solving the puzzle before Patricia.

"Welcome to France," said Patricia with a huge smile as she pointed out the window at the green French countryside.

"What?" Said Mo as she now looked out the window and her blue eyes opened wider. "You mean we *already* went through that tunnel thing?"

"Oh, yes. About fifteen minutes ago." Said Patricia with a laugh while looking down at her watch.

"You sneak," laughed Mo in relief as she softly hit her friend on the arm. "You fooled me with this game."

"Yes, I did," smiled Patricia in return. "Luckily, as we are flying home from Rome, I won't have to think up another distraction for a return trip on the *Eurostar*."

Fifteen minutes after exiting the *Eurostar* at the Paris *Gare du Nord* station, their Mercedes taxi pulled up in front of the *Ritz Hotel* located in the historic *Place Vendome* which was designed in 1702.

Patricia felt like a little schoolgirl about to enter her first birthday party. On the taxi ride from the train station to the hotel, she had already caught several glimpses of the *Eiffel Tower* framed by a deep blue Parisian sky.

Now, she was entering the *Place Vendome* and pulling up in front of the hotel she had dreamed of seeing since she first watched *How to Steal a Million*, with her mom when she was ten years of age.

As they rolled to a stop, her smile and excitement only grew.

A crisply uniformed middle-aged bellman from the Ritz quickly opened the door of the taxi for them, esçorted them out, then went to the trunk to remove their luggage. As he did, Patricia leaned in to pay the driver. Before he even drove away, Patricia had already walked several yards away from the hotel to look up excitedly at its windows.

As she did, Mo looked at the bellman and patted his shoulder. "We will be right with you. My friend is experiencing a magical moment."

And indeed, she was. Patricia looked up at the windows and tried to imagine the room *Simon Dermott* – as played by

Peter O'Toole – stayed in as he came to first help, and then fall in-love with, *Nicole Bonnet* – as played by Audrey Hepburn.

It was from that window that the *Simon Dermott* character practiced throwing his toy boomerang in front of the 144-foot-tall column in the center of the square commissioned by Napoleon in 1810 and built in part, from melted down enemy cannons.

Patricia wanted to book that exact room facing the column or at least one close, but the cost was well beyond anything she had ever imagined. As it was, the smallest and lowest price room offered by *The Ritz* which she did get for their three nights in Paris, was eating up the majority of her entire budget.

But for Patricia, to stay in the most famous and luxurious hotel in Paris was a price literally worth paying as that was the whole point of this trip and this adventure.

Chapter Twenty-Four

Ten minutes after the taxi dropped them off at the Ritz, Patricia and Mo were once again standing in front of the hotel after dropping off their luggage in their room and freshening up.

"Now what, fearless leader?" Asked Mo as she looked at the enormous square before her ringed by designer-name stores and boutiques.

"Now," answered Patricia with a gleam in her eyes. "We are off to – as *Simon Dermott* says in the movie – 'Case the joint.'"

"And just what 'joint' exactly, are we casing?"

"Well," said Patricia as she started to walk toward the *Rue Saint Honore*. "That's an interesting question."

Having no idea where they were going, Mo fell in step next to Patricia who continued to talk.

"In the movie – as I am sure you *don't* remember..."

Mo stuck her tongue out at her friend.

"...Nicole convinces Simon that they have to steal the Cellini Venus from the Claybert-Lafayette Museum. Of course, in reality, that was a fictional name for the museum. William Wyler, who was the famous director of the movie, actually used two *real* museums to substitute for the *one* fictional museum. The first, where they shot all the exterior scenes and where the French police keep driving up every time the obnoxiously loud alarm kept going off, was really *The Musee Carnavalet*, located at 16 Rue des Francs Bourgeois. The museum where the film studio copied some of the interiors to use on the set being *The Musee Jacquemart-Andre* located at 158 Boulevard Haussmann."

"Great," answered Mo as she tried to digest all of that background. "Are we going to both, now?"

Patricia shook her head as the smile which appeared on her face when they arrived, was still there. "No. For the purposes of this adventure, we are only going to *The Musee Carnavalet*. And then from there to *Maxim's*, located at 3 Rue Royale."

"Sorry," said Mo as she lightly laughed. "I know I should have done my homework, but why *Maxim's*?"

Nothing was going to knock the smile off Patricia's face. "That's okay. I didn't expect you to research or remember the movie. One of us being *totally* obsessed is more than enough."

Mo hugged her friend around the shoulders as she smiled. "You are not obsessed. Just more classically and clinically *depressed*."

"In that case," smiled Patricia right back. "It's good to have my keeper along with me. Now, as I was saying, we are going to *Maxim's* for three reasons. First, because it is one of the very best and most famous restaurants in the world. Second – and relevant to this adventure – that is where *Nicole* met both *Davis Leland* – as played by Eli Wallach – and *Simon Dermott*."

"That's what I figured but now I know those movie factoids as well..."

Mo then stopped and tugged at Patricia's elbow. "...Also, are we *walking* all the way to these places?"

Patricia waved her right arm to showcase all that was around them. "Are you kidding? *Look* where we are. Look where *you* are. Leaving my obsession aside, you are in one of the most historic and beautiful cities in the world. A city which begs to be walked so one can take in all its splendor."

Mo shrugged her shoulders. "Splendor or not, I got a blister on the heel of my right foot from walking all over London and I don't want it to start hurting again."

"Don't worry, baby. I have *Band-Aids* and *Neosporin* in my purse if you need it."

Chapter Twenty-Five

Patricia was thrilled to see that after buying their tickets, they still had about two hours to walk around – and "case" – the historic *Musee Carnavalet.*

After walking into one of the over one hundred rooms of the museum, Patricia gently pulled Maureen off to one side out of the way of the other tourists navigating the seemingly endless history and art.

"Yes?" Asked Mo as she watched Patricia start to fish something out of her purse.

Patricia pulled yet another small booklet out of her bag of information.

"I just want to read you a quick paragraph about this museum before we…" She then lowered her voice to whisper. "…*case the joint.*"

Mo was much more interested to learn how the Red Sox were faring in their four-game series against the Yankees now taking place back in Boston, than she was about the history of the museum, but her love for Patricia and her loyalty to her at her time of need superseded everything and demanded her full attention.

"Let me have it," smiled Mo whose long blonde hair was in a ponytail which she adjusted to pull it away from the collar of her green "Green Monstah" t-shirt. "I am all ears."

Patricia knew her friend had little or no interest in the museum and was simply being her best buddy in life. That said, Patricia was still going to read her the paragraph about the museum because it would help to calm her own nerves a little as she tried not to contemplate the utter craziness of her plan.

"Okay," smiled Patricia. "Thank you for pretending to care…"

Mo reached out and touched her friend on the back of her right hand which was holding the booklet.

"I am not pretending, Sweetie. Museums, ballets, operas, and overall 'classy' activities may not be my thing, but at this moment, nothing could be more important to me. *Nothing.* I am here for you and I'm having an incredibly fabulous time."

Patricia took a deep breath to stop herself from becoming emotional again as she quickly hugged Mo around the shoulders.

"Thank you…"

Despite her best efforts, Patricia was worried she might start misting again, so jumped into reading the text.

"*…Situated in the historic Marais district, the Musee Carnavalet is dedicated to the history of Paris from its origins to the present time. Opened in 1880, the museum now occupies two mansions from the 16th and 17th centuries. In this* *remarkable architectural setting, you can discover medieval and Gallo-Roman archeological collections, mementos of the French Revolution, thousands of paintings from the periods, sculptures, furniture from the time, and other priceless works of art."*

"Wow," said Mo. "That sounds really impressive. Except we are not *really* here to 'discover' any of those things, are we? We are here to case the joint."

Patricia looked around the room quickly to see who was nearby then held her left index finger to her lips.

"Sssssssshhhhhhhhh."

"Sorry," answered Mo now in a whisper.

"That's okay. Let's start exploring the museum now... quietly."

They then joined the river of mostly tourists—with the occasional Parisian sprinkled in—winding its way through the breathtaking history of the place and in spite of Patricia's ultimate plan, rightfully found themselves marveling at the works of art they encountered.

As they walked from room to room, Patricia was trying to find a utility closet to eventually hide in like the one used by Simon and Nicole in the movie. While she was disappointed she could not find one, she was very happy when she felt she found the next best thing.

In *How to steal a Million*, just before they hide together in the utility closet inside the museum, Simon pushes Nicole into a huge fireplace and then quickly joins her where they are shielded by a decorative screen in front of it.

As Patricia and Mo walked into a beautiful wood paneled room of the museum, she spotted "Plan B" at the far end.

As in the movie, it was a huge fireplace covered also with a decorative screen. In this case, black in color.

In her excitement of seeing it, Patricia almost jogged across the diagonal-square patterned hardwood floor of the room.

"What happened to playing it cool?" Asked Mo when she caught up with her.

Patricia looked back toward the entrance and then around the room. "Whoops. Sorry about that. Just happy to find this huge fireplace in this room."

"Obviously," smiled Mo.

Just then, a blue-suited guard for the museum came walking into the room. Patricia was almost paralyzed with fear when she realized he was walking straight toward them.

"Hello," he said in heavily French-accented English as he stood in front of them. "I have been looking for you two."

Chapter Twenty-Six

Patricia, whose nerves were pretty much already shot by all the stress from the firm and at home, instantly felt a drop of sweat roll down her back with the announcement from the museum guard.

Mo quickly stole a glance at her friend and realized that she was in no state to speak.

In a protective gesture, Mo stepped closer to the guard. "You have been looking for us, have you?" Said Mo as she arched her eyebrows. "Why?"

The thirty-something, taller than average guard who clearly worked out, looked at them for a moment through his wire-rimmed glasses and then smiled as he pointed to Mo's shirt. "The Green Monster. I love it."

"Pardon me?" asked Mo as she looked down at her green t-shirt with the white lettering.

"Your shirt," pointed the guard. "It is about Fenway Park in Boston, no?"

"No…I mean…Yes, it is," smiled Mo with some relief. "It's the name of the 37-foot-tall wall out in left field at Fenway Park where the Red Sox play. It says, '*Green Monstah*" on my shirt as a joke pronunciation because *we* Bostonians are known for not pronouncing our 'R's.'"

"I know," said the guard as he nodded his head. "I have a cousin who lives in Boston, and he took me to Fenway Park once."

Mo patted the guard on his arm. "Well, that's just great. Wonderful. Thank you for telling us."

Mo then turned and grabbed the still paralyzed by fear Patricia by the arm and started to walk away. They got two feet before the guard tapped Mo on the shoulder.

Mo stopped and turned to see the smiling face of the guard.

"Do you think," he began. "If I give you some money and my address, you could buy me that shirt when you get back and send it to me?"

Mo started to look the guard up and down. "Tell you what. Take off your hat for a minute and let me see what you look like."

Patricia was still turned away from the guard and Mo.

"*What are you doing*?" She instantly whispered through compressed lips.

Mo ignored her friend as she looked at the guard who had now taken his hat off to reveal a thick head of brown hair complementing his very kind face.

Mo nodded. "Very cute. Okay, write down your name, your address, and your email, and I will send you a shirt..."

She then looked him up and down again.

"...I am guessing your size is large."

The guard smiled and nodded, and Mo giggled with his response.

As this was going on, Patricia was beginning to feel faint.

When he finished writing in a small notebook, the guard tore out the page and handed it to Mo.

Mo read it and looked up at the guard. "I'm sorry. I can't quite read your writing. What is your first name?"

"Ro-bare" he said with his heavy French accent.

"What? Oh," nodded Mo. "Robert."

"Yes," answered the now happy guard. "Ro-bare."

Mo looked him in the eyes. "Well, you look like a '*Bobby*' to me, so that's what I'm going to call you. 'Bobby.'"

"*Boo-by*." Responded the museum guard with a smile. "I like that."

He then offered his hand for Mo to shake which she did warmly.

The guard then offered his hand to Patricia who was still turned away from them and not looking.

"Bobby wants to shake your hand, Sweetie." Laughed Mo

Patricia extended her right hand backwards without looking.

The guard looked at Mo who shrugged back at him with a smile.

"She's shy."

The guard nodded as he looked at the back of Patricia's head and then shook her extended hand. As he did so, he noticed it was trembling slightly.

He then stepped back, bowed at Mo and slowly walked into the next room. Just as he was about to disappear around a corner, he paused and took one more fleeting look at them.

As soon as he was out of sight, he took out his little notebook again, and wrote something quickly in it.

Back in the wood paneled room with a stunningly ornate and bright crystal chandelier in its center, and the large fireplace at the far end framed by two masterpieces and a huge 17th Century mirror, Patricia was not feeling very well at all.

She quickly walked behind a red velvet rope and sat in a chair from the Palace of Louis XIV of France.

Mo looked at the red velvet rope and then down at her friend.

"Even though you look all '*Givenchy*' and everything, I don't think you are allowed to sit in those chairs. If the guard comes back, it's the *Bastille prison* for you."

Patricia looked up at Mo and smiled. "First, if I didn't sit down right this second, I was going to *fall* down. Second, I am proud of you for knowing about the *Bastille*."

"Give me a break," laughed Mo. "I've seen *Les Miserables* at least twice in Boston and once even on Broadway."

"Impressive," smiled Patricia. "Education by Broadway musical. That's one way I suppose."

"Yes...*Nicole*," laughed Mo. "So, I'm not as civilized and sophisticated as you and *Simon Dermott*. But at least I'm not a *burglar*."

"Sssssshhhhh," implored Patricia again as she tried to steady herself on the chair. "No one's a burglar...except of course, *Simon Dermott* in the movie – sort of. Anyway, we are just recreating certain scenes from a few movies."

"Yeah," sneered Mo. "Keep telling yourself that when the French judicial system sends us to *Devil's Island* for the rest of our lives."

Before Patricia could respond, Mo continued.

"Yeah, that's right. Mo knows movies. I also saw *Papillon* starring Steve McQueen and Dustin Hoffman, so I know *all about* Devil's Island."

Patricia burst out laughing and stood to hug her friend who was clearly trying to keep her relaxed.

"What's next? Education by comic books?"

Mo stepped back and crossed her arms.

"Hey. Don't knock it. Have you even read an *Archie* comic book or a *Batman* comic book? Trust me, there's a lot you can learn from reading them. Sometimes more than *Vogue* and those other fashion magazines you like to read."

"Maybe there is." Said Patricia. "Come on. I'm feeling much better thanks to you so let's go feed you a light dinner as a reward for your good deed."

Mo nodded her head as she started to walk with Patricia.

"Great. But why a *light* dinner? I'm hungry."

"Because," answered Patricia as she tried not to look suspicious walking out of the museum. "A light dinner at *Maxim's* is all our budget can handle. For a full dinner there, we would have to wait for a shipment of gold bars from Fort Knox."

Chapter Twenty-Seven

Maxim's was everything Patricia had hoped for and more…including the prices.

At something over an average of 200 Euros per person for dinner in the restaurant, Patricia made the executive decision that they would have appetizers at the bar instead. Even at that, she was fairly certain she was going to have to dig around in the bottom of her purse for loose change to help pay the bill.

As they sat at the bar with Patricia sipping from a small glass of Chardonnay and Mo from a glass of Coke and ice, Patricia leaned over to whisper to her friend.

"I am going to walk to the restroom."

Mo leaned back on her bar stool and laughed. "I don't think you have to whisper something like that. I believe that the French, even as worldly and refined as they are, still have to use the facilities from time to time. Very *human being* you know."

"I know that," answered Patricia as her dark eyes took in every detail of the famous bistro. "It's just an excuse to walk around the place and check it out since we are not having dinner in the main restaurant."

Mo then waved in the general direction of the restrooms. "Then by all means, off you go on your world tour of *Maxim's*."

"I will," Patricia nodded. "But first, a little history of this place."

Mo smiled with a feeling of pure love as she watched her BFF reach into her purse for yet another brochure. Mo knew the trip was silly but also understood that buying into the fantasy of the trip and the mental escape and distraction it provided was essential to her friend at the moment.

As Mo had told Patricia from the beginning, she was not that far behind her when it came to being lonely, scared, uncertain, and confused. Life was certainly not turning out to be the bowl of cherries she hoped it would be when she was a little girl.

But Mo also knew that she and Patricia had different personalities with different issues and therefore processed things differently. Mo was much more of a free spirit and tended to let most things roll off her back whereas Patricia was much more sensitive and tended to internalize the hardships of life.

Mo also understood that her job – at least the one she had before "the Silver Skunk" fired her – as difficult and taxing as it had been, was still exponentially easier than the abuse Patricia had been subjected to for years at the firm.

And finally, Mo knew that while her personal life was not remotely where she wanted it to be, her family life was much better than what Patricia had to deal with on a regular basis at home. Mo was very grateful that her mom and dad were still happily married, healthy, and living just ten miles or so away in the town of Westwood, Massachusetts.

Finally, Mo knew that if the situation were reversed, and Mo asked Patricia to go on the silliest of trips or do something seemingly ridiculous to help her mental wellbeing, her friend would do so every single time, no questions asked, and with the biggest of smiles on her face.

Knowing all of that, Mo knew she was exactly where she was supposed to be doing exactly what she should be doing to help the most wonderful and giving person she had ever met.

"Hey, PR.," laughed Mo. "If you know me, you know I can't get enough history or background on any of these places so enlighten me...*please*."

"Thank you," said Patricia. "This will be the last one until we get to Rome."

"Last one. Hundredth one. It's all good. I'm learning something aren't I?"

"Well," smiled Patricia. "You *are*, actually. Even if my reports are not as interesting to you as the final scores for the Red Sox, Patriots, Bruins, or Celtics. Oh, and by the way... they *swept*."

"What?" Asked a now confused Mo.

"The Red Sox. They swept the Yankees. *Swept* is the correct term is it not?"

"It is," laughed Mo. "If the Red Sox won all four games of the series."

"They did." Answered Patricia as she arched her dark and full eyebrows. "I heard a tourist mention it outside of the museum. *See.* I can learn things. 'Swept' means more than just cleaning the kitchen floor."

"Good for you," said Mo as her eyes narrowed. "But don't start quoting me the 40 yard-dash times of the Patriots wide-outs or I'll start to worry about you."

"The 40 who-whats?"

"That's better," smiled Mo. "Now tell me the background of this little greasy spoon."

Patricia perked up as she laid the brochure flat on the bar before her and began to real aloud.

"The legend of Maxim's began in 1893 when Maxime Gaillard, a simple waiter, opened a bistro at number 3 Rue Royale in Paris. Unfortunately, he eventually had money problems and handed the keys over to Eugene Cornuche. Mr. Cornuche then truly turned Maxim's into the Art Nouveau masterpiece it is today. He did so by way of his beautiful "Courtesans." Said Mr. Cornuche at the time: "An empty room? Never. I always have a beauty sitting by the front window in view from the sidewalk." Whatever he did, it worked. Soon, Maxim's became the place to see and be seen. Royalty, the ultra-wealthy, politicians, actors, singers, painters and all in-between made it the most popular eatery in the world. Today, it is owned by the immensely talented and creative Pierre Cardin."

"Wow." Said Mo. "No wonder they can get away with charging thirty dollars for a breadstick."

"They *do not* charge that much."

"Easy, *Mrs. Maxim.* It's only a joke. Now go for your stroll to the *loo* and report back to me."

Patricia nodded and practically skipped all the way to the restroom. Five minutes later, she was back and almost out of breath.

"What's wrong?" Asked Mo.

"I think…I saw it," answered a clearly excited Patricia.

"You think you saw *what*?"

"I think," answered Patricia as she pointed toward the dining room of the restaurant. "I just saw and walked past the actual table used by Audrey Hepburn, Peter O'Toole, and Eli Wallach during the filming of the movie."

Mo was honestly very happy for her friend. If this was going to make her smile and forget some of her pain back home, Mo was buying in totally.

"That's great, Sweetie. Why don't we come back here on our last night and reserve that table for an actual dinner."

Patricia was continually moved by the kindness and thoughtfulness of her friend.

"No. That's okay. I reached over and touched the table and the booth on my way back here and that's more than good enough for me. Now let's order our one breadstick for dinner – which we will be splitting – and then head back to the Ritz."

Chapter Twenty-Eight

5:15 PM the next evening—after a day spent sightseeing, which included stops at the *Louvre* and the *Eiffel Tower* – found Patricia hyperventilating outside of the main entrance to the *Musee Carnavalet.*

As she paced back and forth like a caged tiger in front of the museum, Mo casually walked up and blocked her path.

Patricia, dressed as much as possible *exactly* like Audrey Hepburn's character *Nicole* the evening she hid out in the museum, was wearing a knee-length *Givenchy* knock-off one-piece beige dress with a double-layered skirt, a backwards collar, beige buttons all along the back, and draped pockets. All nicely pulled together by a narrow black belt.

She was staring down intently at her matching beige pumps when Mo interrupted her pacing.

"What are you doing?" Asked Patricia. "You are in my way."

"Precisely." Answered Mo in a more assertive voice. "For a girl who does not want to draw attention to herself, you could have fooled me."

"Why?"

"Why? You ask me, *why*? Well I'll tell you why. Because look at you. You are pacing back and forth so much your heels are digging a trench in the sidewalk. And more than that, you are most likely giving the guards watching through that camera..." Mo then jerked her head in the general direction of one of the security cameras positioned at the entrance of the museum.

"...more than an eyeful as they try to figure out if you are engaging in spontaneous exercise or having a nervous breakdown."

"Both," laughed Patricia as the tension of the moment was once again broken by her best friend.

"Okay," continued Mo who was surprised at how clam she was considering what they were about to do. "Are we going in or not? You look *much* too beautiful in that *Givenchy*-inspired outfit not to get arrested in it and then make it onto the front page of Le *Figaro* tomorrow morning."

"Ha, ha." Answered Patricia who was not at all surprised at how calm her friend was acting. "We are going in."

"Good," smiled Mo. "In that case, I get to quote a line Peter O'Toole says in the movie which I actually memorized last night while you were out walking around the *Place Vendome* at midnight."

This did catch Patricia by surprise. "And what might that be?"

"Ready," said Mo. "First, you have to try and imagine me saying this in Peter O'Toole's voice."

"I will try my hardest." Giggled Patricia.

"Okay...here it comes..." said Mo as she tried to lower the tone of her voice. "*...I want you to take a long last look at the blue sky, the green grass, the trees, and the river. All of which I loathe personally, which is why a juicy stretch in a cozy French prison doesn't bother me at all.*"

Mo then bowed at the waist after delivering her line.

Patricia quickly applauded and then hugged her friend.

"Marvelous. Just marvelous. I am not only proud of you for memorizing the line, but so grateful to you for humoring me in my hour of need."

"My pleasure, Sweetie. Happy to do it. Especially since the French prison part is most likely about to come true."

"Stop that," said Patricia as she took a deep breath and did look around one last time at least at the blue sky, the trees, and the pedestrians and traffic going by. "Okay. Let's do this."

At 5:55 PM – just five minutes before the museum was scheduled to close—Patricia and Mo walked back into the wood paneled room with the large fireplace at the far end.

As the last few minutes ticked away, Patricia and Mo slowly mingled their way to a position right next to the fireplace.

From her vantage point, Patricia could just see into the fireplace behind the large black screen in front of it and could tell that it seemed to have enough room to accommodate them.

A few seconds after making that observation, the bell sounded announcing the closing of the museum. After it did, the five other people still with them in the room quickly made their way toward the exit.

As they did, Patricia took another deep breath, let it out slowly, looked around to make sure no one was coming, and then gently pushed Mo toward the fireplace.

"Stop shoving me," whispered Mo.

"I not shoving you," whispered Patricia back. "I'm gently guiding you. Now please get in the fireplace."

Mo shook her head. "I don't think we have properly thought this one through."

Patricia pushed her again with pleading eyes. It was the pleading eyes which got to Mo.

"Okay. Okay," smiled Mo. "Stop with the sad cow eyes. I'm going already."

With that, Mo took her own deep breath and then squeezed herself behind the screen and into the fireplace.

As Patricia quickly walked to the other side of the screen to enter that way, Mo's head suddenly popped up in the middle of the screen like a *Whack-a-Mole.*

Patricia shoved Mo's head back down and then slid in past the screen next to her in the fireplace.

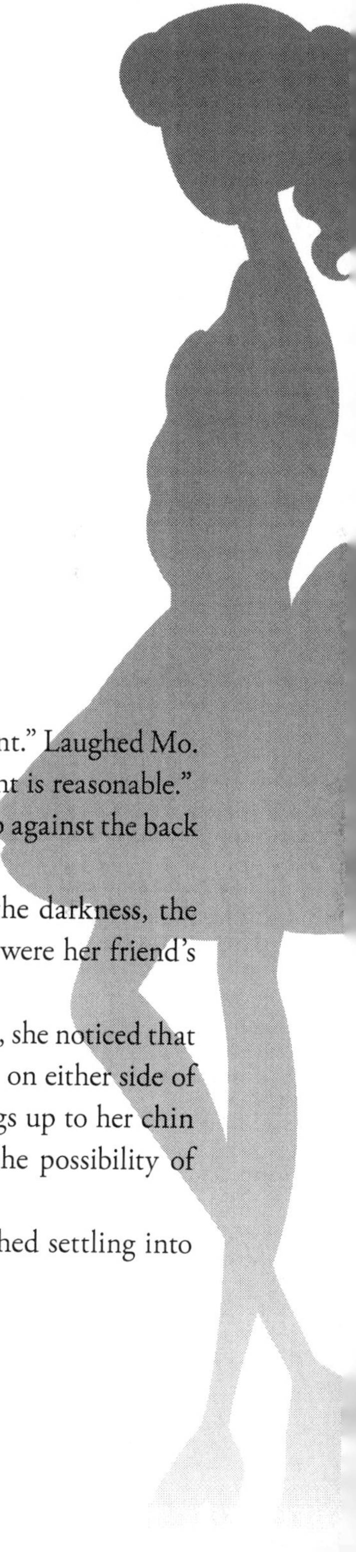

Chapter Twenty-Nine

"Welcome to my little Parisian apartment." Laughed Mo. "It's not much to look at but the rent is reasonable."

Mo was sitting with her back propped-up against the back of the fireplace.

At least until her eyes could adjust to the darkness, the only thing Patricia could clearly make out, were her friend's legs from the knees down.

Patricia slipped in next to Mo. As she did, she noticed that they each only had about six inches of room on either side of them and that she had to almost pull her legs up to her chin to keep her feet away from the screen or the possibility of someone seeing them.

"Comfy?" Asked Mo after Patricia finished settling into position.

"Ssssshhhhh," answered Patricia.

Mo next pulled her iPhone out of her purse and clicked it on. As soon as she did, she and Patricia were bathed in a bright white light.

Patricia reached over and instantly snatched the phone out of Mo's hand and pushed the button to turn it off.

"Are you mad?" She whispered as they were once again sitting in the dark.

"Sorry," answered Mo. "I just wanted to note the time we entered the Bat Cave."

"About thirty seconds ago," Patricia whispered even more softly. "Besides, my watch face glows in the dark, so please don't do that again."

"Now what?" Asked Mo in a volume which now matched Patricia's.

"Now…we wait a few minutes, listen, and be very, very quiet."

"Why?" Giggled Mo. "Are we hunting *Wabbits*, Elmer Fudd?"

"What is *wrong* with you?" Asked Patricia as she shook her now giggling friend's knee.

"I don't know," answered Mo as she continued to softly laugh. "I think the craziness of all of this is making me insane."

"I understand," nodded Patricia in the darkness. "Just please slip into your insanity in silence."

No sooner had she whispered those words then they heard footsteps entering the room. By the sound of it, Patricia guessed it was two male guards talking to each other as they made a casual sweep of the room.

At least she hoped it was casual.

After another five seconds or so, the footsteps and the voices moved on to another part of the museum.

Not only was Patricia in shock that they had gone through with her crazy stunt, but that so far, it seemed to be working.

After thirty minutes or so of sitting motionless and quiet, Mo finally spoke up again.

"PR," said Mo in her new and improved very low volume. "Remember how I said that maybe this caper was not thought through properly?"

"Yes."

"I want to now add to that concern with a dose of reality."

"Which is what?"

"Which is...," answered Mo with a waver to her voice. "... that I had three cups of coffee in the café at the Ritz during and after our late lunch. Now, as you know, coffee goes right through me..."

"TMI...," interrupted Patricia.

"TMI or not," answered Mo with a small laugh. "It's a reality. And unless there is a bathroom in this fireplace, we are soon going to have an emergency to deal with."

"Hah," said Patricia in a triumphant whisper. "Actually, contrary to *someone's* somewhat ignorant remarks, I *did* think things through."

That statement made, Patricia quietly reached into her purse and started to remove a few objects and put them on her lap. When she was finished, she turned on a tiny little flashlight to show Mo her supplies of the moment.

Mo looked down at Patricia's lap to see two small bottles of water from the *Ritz*, two packs of crackers from *Maxim's*, and…

"Are those," asked Mo as her eyes went wide. "What I *think* they are?"

"Well," said Patricia with quick laugh. "They are if you happen to think they are disposable diapers."

Mo looked down in amazement at the two diapers encased in a plastic bag along with a handful of paper napkins.

"If you think," announced Mo in a voice that was rising by the second. "That I am going to put on a disposable diaper while hiding in a fireplace in this museum, then you have finally crossed the last threshold into crazy-town."

Patricia reached over and covered Mo's mouth with her hand.

"Sssssshhhhhh. Do you want us to get caught?"

"I dmmmmffff pppmmmmmfff…"

"What?" Asked Patricia before realizing her hand was still covering Mo's mouth and removed it.

"I said," answered Mo while trying to catch her breath. "That I do if it means I can use a real bathroom in a French prison instead of an adult diaper."

"Oh," said Patricia who instantly went quiet as she snapped off the tiny flashlight.

After a minute of the two of them once again sitting in the dark, Mo realized that her – at least for the time-being—overly sensitive friend, was truly hurt.

Mo reached over and put her arm around Patricia's shoulders.

"Sorry. I don't want us to get caught. *Really*, I don't. That said, I'll be darned if I struggle out of my jeans, take off my panties and slip on an adult diaper in front of you."

"Then what?" Asked Patricia in a very soft voice.

"Then," laughed Mo. "It looks like I may have to set the world record for 'holding it' until we get out of here."

"Thank you," answered a happier Patricia. "You are the best."

"Well," laughed Mo. "That's actually true so spread the word."

Chapter Thirty

"C*ramp, cramp, cramp, cramp*," yelled Mo forty-five minutes later as she grabbed her right calf and began thrashing about inside the fireplace.

"You're kicking the screen," whispered Patricia as loud as she dared.

"*Ouch, ouch, ouch, ouch*," yelled Mo even more loudly.

As Mo started to bounce around the fireplace from the growingly intense pain, Patricia wrapped her arms around her friend to stop her from moving.

It didn't help.

"*My calf, my calf, my calf, my calf*," cried Mo as she tried to free herself from Patricia's grip in an effort to stop the knot from forming in her right calf.

As Mo was struggling with her and yelping at the same time, Patricia heard a loud crash.

By the time she realized it was the large black screen getting knocked over – as in the one that was keeping them hidden – she and Mo had rolled collectively ten feet out into the room.

As soon as they came to a stop, a very loud alarm started to ring.

"Whoops," said Patricia into Mo's ear as they were still both entangled on the floor.

"Whoops, what?" Asked Mo who was thrilled to be able to extend her right leg fully and lessen the intense pain.

"I forgot," answered Patricia as she also now noticed red lights flashing around the museum in unison with the alarm. "That back in 1966, Peter O'Toole's character *Simon Dermott* never had to deal with motion detectors and heat sensors when he popped out of the closet to throw his toy boomerang in the museum."

"Yeah," said Mo. "Probably something we both should have known *before* we snuck into the fireplace of a tightly guarded museum."

Just as Mo finished the sentence, she and Patricia were picked up off the floor by several very strong hands.

Now in the upright and locked position, Patricia and Mo were staring at four museum guards who looked anything but amused.

One of them being the guard who had spoken with Mo the day before about her t-shirt.

"Oh, hi, *Bobby*." Said Mo with a big smile.

The three other guards looked at Robert and started to quickly address him in French. He answered back in an even more animated fashion.

As he was doing that, four French policemen walked into the room to join the four museum guards and Patricia and Mo.

A few seconds later, Robert took Mo by the arm.

"May I speak with you for a moment in the next room?"

Mo smiled even larger as she followed the guard into the next room of the museum.

As they were gone, Patricia tried to get her breathing under control while smoothing down her dress and trying to not make eye contact with the seven large and uniformed men still in the room with her.

As they did not consider her a threat, they were continually turning their heads from her to the other room trying to figure out what was going on there.

After another two minutes or so of grumbling between the guards and police, Mo and Robert walked back into the room.

As soon as they did, Robert motioned the three other guards and the four French policemen over to him.

As the others now clustered around Robert, Mo quickly walked over to Patricia.

"Bobby wants to let us go."

"What?" Asked Patricia who barely had the mental capacity to speak.

"For real. Turns out, he's the supervisor of the guards and tonight he is on the 4 PM to Midnight shift. I explained to him that you are a little crazy in the head and on heavy medication and that sometimes you like to pretend you are Audrey Hepburn and that you talked me into hiding in the fireplace for a few minutes to recreate a movie scene and then we both fell asleep and were trapped in the museum after hours."

"You told him I was *crazy*?"

"It was the first thing that came to my mind."

"Thanks," said Patricia now looking down at the floor. "That makes it even worse."

"PR," said Mo in a now stronger voice. "We both know it's not true and if it gets us out of here, who cares."

"Maybe I am crazy. I don't know anymore."

"Oh, stop it," insisted Mo as she hugged her friend again around the shoulders. "You're the furthest thing from crazy. You were just way over-worked, way over-stressed and desperate for a little happiness and normalcy. This trip is *exactly* what the doctor ordered."

As Mo was saying that, Robert, the guards, and the police were all having a vigorous discussion morphing into an argument on the other side of the room.

After another minute or so, it subsided with a now smiling Robert walking back over to Patricia and Mo.

"It was not easy," smiled the guard with the kind face as he looked at Mo. "But I have convinced my colleagues and the Police to let you both go…under one condition."

"And what might that be?" Asked Mo as she once again raised her blonde eyebrows.

"That you have a cup of coffee with me after my shift is over tonight and at least lunch with me tomorrow before I have to report back to the museum."

Mo broke out in a huge smile then instantly tried to cover it as she suddenly felt guilty over having something so nice happen to her in front of her friend who had been through so much of late.

"That is very sweet of you, but I don't think..." Mo began to say before she was interrupted by Patricia.

"I think that is simply a wonderful idea. Just as I think it will be rude of you not to accept Robert's invitation after he has gotten us out of all the trouble I created."

Mo shook her head. "No, my place is with you."

Patricia turned fully to face Mo and took both of her hands in hers.

When she did, Mo saw the tears forming combined with strangest look of both hopelessness and happiness in her eyes.

"Please," said Patricia as she held her friend's hands ever tighter. "It's okay. It will *truly* make me so very happy if you do this. Besides that, I think I need to be alone now for a few days."

"PR. I am not going to leave you al..."

"*Please,*" begged Patricia in a tone of complete despair Mo had never heard come out of her before. "*Please.* We are paid up at the Ritz for one more night and I will talk to Cheryl about finding you a room for the next few nights just in case you need more time in Paris."

Mo's mind was reeling as she tried to process what was happening. Not knowing what to do or say, her mind and body decided some role reversal crying was the best response as she hugged her best friend in life.

Patricia gently stroked the back of Mo's head while she sought out eye contact with Robert.

When she found it, he smiled at her, nodded his head, and whispered, "*I will keep her safe. I promise.*"

After a few more seconds, Patricia stepped back from Mo so she could once again look her squarely in the eye.

"Look. I *will* be okay. Really, I will. I am going to take a long walk right now if that's okay with you and then make arrangements to take the *Rail-Europe* train to Rome first thing in the morning."

Mo looked at Robert whose face seemed even more kind and caring now, then back at Patricia.

"Are you sure, Sweetie?"

"I am very sure," said Patricia as she wiped her eyes with a tissue. "We will meet in Rome in a few days…"

She then looked at Robert and back at Mo. "I can't wait to hear your stories when you get there."

Patricia then quickly hugged Mo.

When she was done, she stepped over and hugged Robert.

"Thank you." She whispered. "*Please* be a very good person. She needs that more than ever."

"You have my word," answered Robert who was genuinely touched by the hug as well as the deep affection he was witnessing between Mo and Patricia.

After hugging Robert, Patricia walked up to each guard and French policeman, shook their hand, and quietly said, "Thank you so very much for your kindness."

All seven men smiled back at her realizing they were in the presence of true grace.

One of the French policemen walked up to her and offered his arm.

"*Mademoiselle.* It will be our honor to escort you anywhere you need to go."

Chapter Thirty-One

6:15 AM the next morning, Patricia boarded a high-speed TGV train at the *Paris Gare Lyon* station for her trip to Rome after a transfer in Milan.

After leaving the museum, she had gone straight to the *Ritz*, packed her suitcases and walked the short distance to the Westin Hotel where she checked in for her final night in the City of Light.

She honestly was thrilled that her best friend had an opportunity to at least get to know someone who seemed decent and kind. To find such a person in Paris made it all the more special.

Because of that very positive energy, Patricia did not want to detract even one little bit from the moment or the possibilities. With that thought in mind, she left a note for Mo on her pillow telling her to text her with updates, that she loved her, and that she would see her in Rome.

A little more than fourteen hours after checking out of the Westin Hotel next to *Place Vendome* in Paris, she checked into the *Intercontinental De La Ville* and soon found herself in one of the most beautiful hotel rooms she had ever seen in a hotel perfectly situated at the top of the Spanish Steps and near all of the treasures of Roma.

During her eleven plus hour train ride from Paris to Rome, Patricia had spent almost the entire journey in personal reflection. To be sure, she knew she was lonely, scared of the uncertainty which awaited her back home, and most likely that she was clinically depressed at times.

That said, toward the end of the train trips, she had one more epiphany. Quite possibly the most important of her life.

That being that she was sick of feeling sorry for herself. Sick of it. It was negative energy and poison which was draining her capacity to find and embrace whatever happiness was out there in a world going madder by the moment.

Patricia *knew* she was on the trip of a lifetime. A trip most people in the real world she inhabited could never afford to take even once in their lives. Everything about it had been magical. From the QM2, to the trains, to the ultra-luxury hotels, to most especially the cities visited. She told herself, to be in London, Paris, and Rome for the first – and maybe only – time in her life and to be miserable, was an insult to all who dreamed of such experiences but could never go for one reason or another.

On top of all of that, she knew she was still blessed with a few good friends – most especially Mo—and a wonderful family. Ultimately, the most precious treasure worth having.

When she got home, she would have to find a job, she would have to deal with family issues, and she might have to accept the very real possibility that she would never find the right man for herself.

She knew all that and after several hours of beating herself up on the trains, was now at peace with whatever came her way.

For now, she was in Rome. *Rome.* The "Eternal" city.

A city she had dreamed of seeing since she was a little girl. A city which was the last leg of a magical trip. A magical trip which had been robbed of much of its enchantment by one thing, and one thing only. Her *own mood* and her own negative energy.

"Well...No More," Patricia declared to herself.

She was in Rome and she was going to enjoy every single second of it for the next few days.

Life was a gift to *live*, and she was determined to restart immediately.

Chapter Thirty-Two

After the best night's sleep she had had in a long time, Patricia ate a light breakfast in the restaurant of the hotel, went back to her room to freshen up, and then planned to head out the front door straight for the famous *Spanish Steps* just yards away.

But then – while waiting to ask one of the desk clerks a question – she decided to walk around the rest of the lobby of the spectacular *Intercontinental De La Ville.* And when she turned the corner into one of the beautiful and ornate sitting rooms of the hotel, her jaw literally dropped open.

For what greeted her, were several large full-color ceramic murals of Audrey Hepburn in some of her most iconic outfits and poses. Patricia was so shocked and delighted with the discovery that she sat in the nearest chair to steady herself as she looked up in wonder at the stunning murals.

"Surely," she thought to herself as she stared in awe at Audrey Hepburn gazing back down at her. "This has to be a sign. It has to *mean* something. Unbeknownst to me, the very hotel I pick in Rome for my 'Channeling Audrey Hepburn' *Roman Holiday* adventure has these beautiful murals of Audrey Hepburn welcoming me to the hotel and to the city she is still most associated with. *Kismet? Karma?* I don't know what it means but I'm taking it for all the positive energy and happiness this 'coincidence' is giving me."

Excitedly, and with apologies to no one, she was now more determined than ever to make today her *Audrey Hepburn-Roman Holiday*-Holiday. Over the course of however many hours it took, she intended to visit every single location she could find where they filmed the 1953 classic for which Hepburn won an Oscar.

For her own *Roman Holiday*-Holiday, Patricia chose to wear the "*Princess Ann*" outfit most identified with the movie. That being the collared, short-sleeved, starched white shirt with the sleeves rolled up even higher, tucked tightly into a full-length sky-blue skirt. Both held in place by the matching four-inch-wide sky blue belt. As accessories, Patricia also wore the red and white scarf around her neck as well as the soft-red Roman sandals.

As she walked around the *Spanish Steps* and tried to pick out the exact spot *Princess Ann* and *Joe Bradley* talked and where the Princess ate her very first ice cream cone, a strange thing began to happen.

At first, the tourists around her began to murmur and subtly point at her. After a few more minutes, a young man walked up and asked if he could have his photo taken with her. Then another. Then two young girls. Then a family. Then two older women.

As the two older women posed with her, one of them turned to face her.

"Are you an actress? Is this part of a publicity campaign?"

"No," smiled Patricia. "Publicity campaign for what?"

"For a remake of Roman Holiday."

"Oh, no." Laughed Patricia. "It is my favorite movie and I just decided to be silly for the day and wear one of the outfits from the film."

"It's remarkable." Said the other woman.

"What is?" Asked Patricia after one of their husbands finished taking a photo with his phone.

"You are the spitting image of Audrey Hepburn. It's as if a colorized version of her just stepped out of the film and is now really here on the Spanish Steps with all of us."

That compliment, along with the unintended consequences of the photo requests, made Patricia a bit self-conscious. After thanking the women for their comments, she quickly walked down the steps to make an escape from the "fifteen-minutes of fame" she was in no way seeking.

But it was not to be.

For the rest of the day, everywhere she stopped on her personal *Roman Holiday* tour – be it on *Via Condotti*, the "home" of Joe Bradley at *Via Margutta 51*, *Trevi Fountain*, *Ponte Sant'Angelo* for the river barge scene, or outside of the *Roman Colosseum*, tourists kept flocking to her to have their photo taken with her.

In fact, it was in the mid-afternoon, when she was standing in front of the *Trevi Fountain*, that a young man with a very expensive looking camera around his neck walked up to her.

"Good afternoon," he said in English with an Italian accent. "Are you from Great Britain?'

"No," smiled Patricia who decided the best way to deal with the unintended attention, was to humor it quickly and move on. "I am from the United States."

"Ah. Okay. So…you are an actress?" He asked with a slight smile.

"No."

"A model."

"No."

"A musician?"

"No." Answered Patricia as she began to laugh.

"Why are you laughing?" Asked the young man with the large camera.

Patricia turned her head to look across the fountain to where they shot the barber shop scene with *Princess Ann*.

"Oh…nothing. Your questions just now created one of those surreal moments of life imitating art."

To Patricia, the young man looked to be in his early twenties. As *Roman Holiday* came out decades before he was even born, she was sure any explanation would be lost on him.

Surprisingly, he asked for none and merely nodded his head in a very knowing way.

"I understand…*Princess*." He smiled. "But I am not *Mario Delani*, the barber. I am a photographer for *Corriere Della Sera*. Do you mind if I take a few photos of you?"

Corriere Della Sera? *Corriere Della Sera*? Thought Patricia. That was the name of the largest and most influential newspaper in Italy.

"Well, you look much too young to be working at such an important newspaper or especially know anything about an old move, but alright. Let the fantasy continue just a little bit longer."

"*Grazie*," said the young man in Italian as he took a flurry of photos in just seconds.

When he was finished, he took out a small notebook.

"May I have your name, please?"

"May I say no." Answered Patricia as she slowly shook her head. "As surreal moments like now and fantasies like today don't really happen, I think it best to remain anonymous."

The young man with the thick mop of black hair looked at her for a few seconds and then took a business card out of his shirt pocket.

"Fair enough. But if you change your mind, my email and phone number are on the card."

"I won't," said Patricia as she took and examined the card. "But thank you for the attention."

"Oh." Laughed the young man as he adjusted his camera and turned to walk away. "It was my pleasure to be sure. *Roman Holiday* is my mother's favorite movie. So, while your name and what you are doing will remain a mystery...for now, I must say, there is something quite...regal about you. *Surreal*, even."

Chapter Thirty-Three

At the end of a very long day, and with the sun soon to set, Patricia was standing in the deep shadow of a building just down the street from the portico of the sixth-century *Church of Santa Maria*.

She was standing in the shadow because she was waiting for the last of the tourists to leave the one *Roman Holiday* filming location she most wanted to see.

That being, *The Mouth of Truth* which was located just inside the portico.

It was at this site, that her favorite part of the movie took place. For that reason, she just wanted the time to enjoy it on her own. No photos, no tourists, no confusion.

She was truly humbled and happy that anyone would want to take her photo, but for now, she just wanted this moment to be hers.

When she finally did walk in, she was thrilled to see that it looked exactly like it did in the film. There was a small stone bench off to the left and just in front of historic artifact made famous by the movie, and with no one in sight, Patricia gratefully sat on its cool surface to give her aching feet a much-needed rest.

As she sat in the still warm portico, she felt her eyelids growing heavy and closed them for just a few moments.

Seconds later, in almost a daze, she felt someone touch her right shoulder.

"Hello, Patricia."

Patricia jumped up off the bench with the touch and the sound of the deep male voice.

When she turned, she was looking up at the smiling face of Tom Harris.

Maybe it was the heat she thought. Or maybe total mental and physical exhaustion. Or maybe, she had just finally snapped and was hallucinating.

"What…how…what…What are you doing *here*? How did you find me?"

Patricia's heart was racing a mile a minute and she wobbled a bit until Tom took her by the shoulders and gently guided her back down to the bench.

He next reached into a computer bag sitting by his feet, pulled out a small bottle of water, opened it, and handed it to her.

She took a long sip, took a few breaths, and then took another long sip.

"Thank you," she said as she handed the bottle back. "How…"

"Well...a little birdie may have tweeted me."

"Mo." Declared Patricia.

"I am not sure if I caught the little birdie's name. Only that she was staying behind in Paris for a few extra days with a *Boo-bie*."

Patricia laughed out loud with the sound creating a slight echo in the chamber.

As she paused to study Harris, she was surprised to see that he was dressed in a charcoal gray suit with a white shirt, and deep blue tie.

"You are all dressed up."

Tom looked down at himself.

"Yeah. I guess I am. It's been a crazy last couple of weeks. A few days after you left, I quit the firm, took my team with me, and then started a new boutique firm. A firm where – by the way—all legal secretaries and non-timekeepers get profit sharing, where they get overtime above forty hours per week, where all overtime is voluntary, and where a legal secretary will be part of the committee overseeing the firm."

"Wow. So, you do *walk the walk* on that one." Said Patricia.

"Yeah," continued Harris who was also beyond exhausted and hoped he was making sense. "And after all of that was up and running, I jumped on the non-stop *Alitalia* fight out of Logan and got in early this morning. I didn't even bring a suitcase, so TSA almost didn't let me fly."

"Oh, I see. So, what have you been doing since this morning?"

"Looking for you."

"Why?" Asked Patricia with a very steady gaze.

Harris chose to ignore the question for the moment and smiled.

"You are famous, you know."

"Pardon me?"

"You have become a certified Internet sensation," answered Harris as he pulled out his iPhone and opened his *Google* portal.

Once he did that, he typed in some letters, waited for an image to appear, and then handed the phone to Patricia.

When Patricia looked at the screen, she was stunned to see a photo of herself on the *Corriere Della Sera* site.

Harris leaned over and pointed at the headline in Italian above the image.

"It says, '***Mysterious Audrey Hepburn-Double Enchants Rome with Her Beauty and Charm***.' It then goes on to ask its readers if they can identify you. The site and the Twitter universe have gone absolutely crazy. It seems everyone now wants to know *who* you are."

"This can't be," said a confused Patricia. "I was just being silly today."

"Silly or not," said Harris as he tapped the screen. "You have captured the imagination of a number of people…me included."

"How did you find me?"

"Actually," answered Harris and he waved his phone. "It was thanks to this story in part. Mo told me what hotel you were staying at but when I got there you were gone. I then tried to call you but there was no answer."

"I left my phone in my room."

"That explains that," smiled Harris. "So, after walking around the city aimlessly for a while, I stopped in a café to take a break. As I did, there was a young Italian couple next to me and the guy was reading *Corriere Della Sera* on his laptop. I about dropped my coffee when I saw *your* photo. The story then mentioned Audrey Hepburn and *Roman Holiday.* Maybe no surprise to you, but there are a bunch of tours in this city which *only* go to the sites where they filmed *Roman Holiday.* I downloaded one, and well…here I am…finally."

"Why?" Asked the suddenly much more confident and secure Patricia. "Won't your *fiancé* be upset?"

"I don't know," said Harris as he shook his head and ran his hand through his hair. "And it no longer matters. I came to a number of decisions after you left. A week or so after you boarded the train at South Station, I called off the engagement and ended our relationship."

"Why did you do that?"

Harris stood and started to pace back and forth in front of her.

"I did it for *me.* I did it because the last few months with Simone have been smothering. Every day, I felt more claustrophobic. Every day, she put the superficial and people's opinion of her and us *before* us and *before* my feelings. I found myself just going along to get along because everyone kept saying what a '*beautiful and perfect couple we were.*' Except… we weren't. Far from it. To this day, I don't think she really cared. She just wanted *her* image of what a '*perfect*' husband would look like on her arm when she trotted me out before her friends or family or at the endless social functions she had us attend in an effort to climb the television anchor ladder. I just didn't know how to get out. I didn't know how to end it. Like so many people in a troubled engagement, I did not want to do the right thing and walk away because I didn't want to offend anyone or waste all the planning that was going into our '*Fairytale*' wedding."

"So, what changed?" asked Patricia in a monotone and guarded voice.

Harris stopped pacing, stood before Patricia, put his fingers under her chin and slowly lifted her face until she was looking at him.

"What changed? Meeting *you*. After our first talk, I was mesmerized. I couldn't wait to see you again. Every free second my mind filled with thoughts about you. After that first day we met in the kitchen at the firm, I laid in bed that night until at least five-thirty in the morning just thinking about you. I couldn't sleep. I didn't *want* to sleep. I just wanted to keep thinking of you and hoping I would have the chance to talk with you more the next day. Nothing like that has ever happened to me before. Suddenly, I wanted to tell you *everything* about me. I wanted you to *know* me. That's why I opened up to you in Boston Common. Obviously, too much. But suddenly, I desperately wanted you to know that it had basically been over for me and Simone for quite some time."

Patricia slowly moved Tom's fingers from under her chin and patted the bench next to her.

"I'm sorry," she said once he sat back down. "But I don't know how to believe you. I don't know how to believe anyone anymore."

Chapter Thirty-Four

Harris thought quickly. He had not come this far and put his heart on display to be rejected now. He looked around the chamber and quickly locked his eyes on something and then broke out in a huge grin.

He jumped up and pointed at the wall.

"Patricia. *Look* where we are. Look *where* I found you. Sitting in front of the *Mouth of Truth*. As explained in *Roman Holiday*, if I put my hand in the mouth and you ask me a question and I *lie*, my hand will be *cut off*."

Harris then ran over and inserted his right hand into the opening of the face.

"Come on," he said with total conviction. "Ask me a question. Ask me if what I just told you is true."

Patricia looked at him, looked at his right arm protruding from the *Mouth of Truth*, and then back at him and started laughing.

Another surreal moment, she thought. As she looked at the incredibly handsome man now standing before her with his hand in the *Mouth of Truth*, her mind flashed for a split-second to the *Joe Bradley* character as played by Gregory Peck, doing the same thing.

"Alright," she began slowly. "I will ask you that question, but two more first."

Harris felt a surge of hope and smiled with her reaction.

"Please."

Patricia stood and walked over to him.

"Okay. Here we go. First, did you *really* quit and start a new law firm?"

"Yes."

"Next, are you truly and honestly now a single man with no attachments whatsoever?"

"Yes."

Patricia smiled as she looked at his arm in the *Mouth of Truth.*

"Is your hand still attached to your arm?"

"Was that the third question?" Asked Tom with a smile.

"No," laughed Patricia. "I just thought of that one. And no leading the witness, counselor."

"Sorry," said Harris. "I think my hand is still there. I can sort of feel my fingers."

"Okay. Last question. And no second chances on this one. Is what you just said about me also completely and totally true?"

Tom knew in the movie, Gregory Peck pulled his arm out of the *Mouth of Truth* and pretended his hand had been cut off. He had no intention of repeating that prank right now.

"I have never," began Harris as he looked into Patricia's beautiful deep brown eyes and almost melted. "Said anything more true, more honest, or more heartfelt in my life."

He then slowly removed his arm from the *Mouth of Truth* and showed Patricia his hand.

After doing so, in the reflected golden glow of the setting sun, Tom slowly leaned over, took Patricia's face gently in his hands, and softly kissed her on the lips.

To his great relief and delight, she kissed him right back.

When they finished, he stepped back and smiled.

"Wow." He whispered.

"Wow." She repeated.

After a few more seconds, he placed both of his hands on her shoulders.

"Is it okay if I now ask you a question?"

"Of course," Patricia answered as she put her hands on his waist.

"As your amazing adventure is just about finished," said Harris as he pulled her closer to him. "Which city on your Audrey Hepburn tour of a lifetime was your favorite?"

"Well," she smiled wider than she had ever smiled in her life. "Thanks to you – and to channel *Princess Ann* one last time—it's Rome. *By all means, Rome. I will cherish my visit here in memory, as long as I live.*"

THE END

About the Author

D. M. MacKinnon is a former principal for an international law firm and a Boston (Dorchester) born author who, as a young writer, had the rare privilege and high honor to not only meet Audrey Hepburn, but assist her with a project. This is the author's first romance novel.

Made in the USA
Middletown, DE
09 September 2023

38245779R00108